# The Memory of Snow
## by
## Kirsty Ferry

**Rosethorn Press**

The Memory of Snow

Copyright © Kirsty Ferry 2012

All rights are reserved. No part of this publication
may be reproduced, stored, or transmitted in any
form or by any means, without prior written
permission of the copyright owner.

----

All characters depicted within this publication, other
than the obvious, historical figures, are fictitious and
any resemblance to any real persons, living or dead is
entirely coincidental.

ISBN-13:978-1511700139

# PROLOGUE

## October 1876

The moon shone over the frosty landscape, gilding everything with unearthly silver. The two men picked their way across the fields, stumbling now and then over ridges in the ground and lumps of stone embedded in the crunchy grass.

'How much further?' hissed the younger man.

'Not far,' replied his companion, a stocky figure silhouetted by the candle-light which spilled out from his miner's lamp. 'It's down here. I saw them working on it.'

'What if they're still about, guarding it or something?'

The older man snorted with laughter. 'Guarding the place? Howay, Tommy. Who's going to nick any of that stuff anyway?'

'But we're nicking...'

'No! We are not nicking stuff. We are liberating stuff. John Clayton's got enough at his place along the road. Truth be told, they say he's been giving it away anyway. You could come and stand around watching like the Lords and Ladies, and be a little begging dog if you want. But this is the man's way of doing it, the lead miner's way.'

'Clayton is eighty four, man! Can we not let him have his little bit of glory, Ralph?'

'Glory? He's had enough of that as well. He's done alright for a town clerk, that man. But it's us, see, who need to find out what's going on up here. I've heard there's some sort of treasure trove. And them archaeologists blokes, they're not working at the weekend, right? So we can take our time. The other lads are comin' later on. I reckon about thirty of them'll come down. We want to get there first. It's kind of like our right anyway– if it wasn't for our lads discovering it, the top blokes would be none the wiser.'

'I don't know, Ralph. It's a bit weird down here. I've heard tales. A lad in Hexham said it was haunted.'

'Rubbish. It's a story they've put about to discourage honest folk like us. They want to hang onto it all for themselves. Ah. Here it is. Look. They've got it all penned off.'

Tommy shuddered and looked around him.'It's spooky, man.'

'It's nigh on midnight in the countryside, Tommy. Nae lights. That's all it is, lad. Come on.' Ralph ducked under the ropes and unfolded his sack. Setting his lamp down on the grass, he peered into the marshy pool before him. Lined with blocks of stone, the water glowed like mercury in the half-light of the moon. A tray lay next to the pool, covered in canvas. Ralph lifted the cover and smacked his lips. 'You little beauties,' he said.

The tray was full of small, round, dirty objects; Roman coins, he was willing to bet. He grabbed a handful of relics from the tray and shoved them into his sack. His contacts had promised this – they said they would sell for quite a few pounds, if he saw the right man in Newcastle.

'I don't know, Ralph. It's just...wrong. We shouldn't be here. Those things were put there for a reason,' whispered Tommy. The place had a queer feel to it, he thought. Not quite right. It felt like they were nicking the lead from the church roof or something.

'These things were put there years ago, mate. Who's going to miss them now? Easy come, easy go,' replied Ralph, scooping another handful out of the tray. 'Do you think they counted these? You reckon they know how many there were?' he asked. 'Not to worry. There'll be plenty more in that Well. Load of old rubbish anyway; bleedin' gods and goddesses and water nymphs.' He laughed. 'More like a dumping ground. Look at it all. We'll get a canny price for these, mate, see if we don't.'

'There's some altars or something, Ralph. Standing up in the field over there. It must be canny deep for them to have put those things in it.' Tommy stood up and shivered, suddenly feeling uncomfortable. 'Come on, I think we've got enough now,' he said, folding over the top of his sack.

'There's tons of stuff!' muttered Ralph, not listening. 'I think there's a box of jewellery over here as well. Oh yes. Come here, my lovelies…' He rummaged through the tray, the pins and brooches cold even against his October fingertips.

'Ah no, you can't take them!' cried Tommy. They're bound to have written that lot down.'

'Ye could be right, my lad,' said Ralph. 'Best to maybe take things they haven't picked out of the water yet. Come on, let's have a dip into it.' He leaned over the Well and stared into it. The water had an oily, muddied cast from this angle. Ralph pulled a face. 'It's ganna be chilly, lad, but it's worth it.' He plunged his hand in up to the elbow and gasped with the cold. The water was so icy it almost burned him. Ralph swore loudly, but churned up the water, groping around for something, anything before he lost all sensation in his arm. His fingers finally closed around something hard and rounded. 'Gotcha, my beauty,' he said, and he pulled the object out of the Well. He shone his lamp over it carefully and scraped the mud off it. Then he screamed.

Clutched in Ralph's hand was a smooth piece of bone; the top of a skull. Globs of mud dropped from it, plopping back into the Well, breaking away from the curved edges which seemed to be the top of the eye sockets

Ralph dropped the thing to the ground, still screaming and the skull rolled towards Tommy, touching him on his foot.

'Aaaah! Aaaah! Get it away!' yelled Tommy, jumping up and down, his lamp swinging wildly from his hands. 'Is it real? What's it doing here? Was it an animal?' Ralph joined in the shrieking, slapping his hand back and forth across his breeches, wiping the mud off and trying to get rid of the sensation of touching the skull. 'I divvn't kna, I divvn't kna!' he kept repeating.

'Ralph, what's that?' howled Tommy. A shadow was breaking away from the area around the Well; a black mass that seemed to swell and grow, morphing into the shape of a man.

'Run!' yelled Ralph. 'Quickly. Get away from it!' He grabbed the sack and his lamp, and leaped over the ropes, shouting back towards Tommy to follow him. Tommy screamed and pelted after Ralph, the pair of them heedless of the uneven ground, stumbling and tripping as they ran away from the Well. The coins bounced around in the sack, but the men did not slow down until they were well away from the dig.

Far behind them, the black mass moved towards the Well and stood over the skull. Then it faded into the moonlit landscape, becoming part of the shadows once more.

# 1649

The white-clad figure knelt by the spring. Around about her, the hills glowed emerald in the lowering light of the Autumn Equinox.

'Blessed Coventina, I thank you on this, our celebration of Mabon. The hours of darkness and hours of daylight are equal, the wheel has turned. Summer is over, but our harvest has been plentiful. Take these offerings and bless my people. I pray to you and the sacred water nymphs, thanking you for our food and asking for your help to carry us through winter, towards Yule and then towards Imbolc and the promise of new life.' The girl threw a handful of grains into the Sacred Well and watched as they swirled and separated, eventually sinking out of sight. 'Please accept these gifts as a sign of my devotion.'

She closed her eyes and trailed her fingers through the clear water, feeling the coolness against her skin. An owl skimmed past her, the air current beneath its beating wings barely moving her fair hair.

As Meggie prayed, the air settled and became still in the little hollow at the bottom of the slope. She opened her eyes and stared around her, aware of the shift in the atmosphere. Her gaze alighted on an uneven mound of earth to the east; an abandoned fort, silent now for twelve hundred years. Fallen debris and stones littered the structure, but here and there, traces of a rampart or a wall jutted out of the grass.

Meggie looked up. The setting sun glinted off something before the earth swallowed it; a figure stood silhouetted on the mound, a cloak appearing to flap around its body. It seemed to be grasping something in its hand; a sword or a weapon of some description. A flash of light bounced off it. Meggie blinked, refocusing her grey eyes on the figure.

The owl swooped past her again. The girl ducked her head as the bird's wings brushed her hair. When she looked back at the mound of earth, the figure had gone.

# SUMMER 1949

The long, hot summer had baked the ground to a husk. Dead, yellow grass covered the hillside, with dusty patches of brown speckling the countryside like a thrush's wing.

In the valley below Carrawburgh Fort, the earth shrank back from the corner of a grey slab. Slowly, inch by inch, it pulled away, exposing three stone altars. Touches of red and green paint clung to the letters carved into the stone.

DEO INV M L ANTONIVS PROCVLVS PRAEF COH I BAT ANTONIANAE VSLM

"To the Invincible God Mithras, Lucius Antonius Proculus, prefect of Antonine's Own First Batavian Cohort willingly and deservedly fulfills his vow."

D IN M S AVL CLVENTIVS HABITVS PREF COH I BATAVORVM DOMV VLTINA COLON SEPT AVR L VSLM

"To the Invincible and Most-Sacred God Mithras, Aulus Cluentius Habitus, prefect of the First Batavian Cohort, of the Ultinian voting tribe, a native of Colonia Septimia Aurelia Larinum, willingly and deservedly fulfills his vow."

DEO INVICTO MITRAE M SIMPLICIVS
SIMPLEX PREF VSLM

"To the Invincible God Mithras, the prefect
Marcus Simplicius Simplex, willingly and
deservedly fulfills his vow."

The sacred water from Coventina's Well had
preserved the temple for centuries; blocked with
offerings, the spring had flooded the ground nearby,
protecting the stone building buried deep in the
marshland.

The temple belonged to the cult of Mithras.
A dark, mysterious place where no sunlight was
allowed. But now, it had decided to expose its
secrets.

# AD 390

Janus shifted position, wriggling his toes inside his leather sandals. This bleak northern territory was one of the worst places in the Empire. He blew on his hands to warm them and frowned as he saw the nailbeds with their blue-ish tinge. He lifted his head and his eyes settled on the Temple to the south west of the fort. Suffering this cold was beyond comprehension; at least Mithras the Sun God could be relied upon to bring warmth to the legions at Carrawburgh.

Janus could see the soldiers moving around the temple from his station on the fort. His friend Marcus had told him he had bought a new altar for the temple. Janus saw two men carrying a rectangular object into the building and smiled as he realised this was the latest addition to the building. It would be dedicated within the next few days. Marcus had described the altar to Janus as they bathed one evening.

'I have requested them to carve rays of light by the head of Mithras. When the Father lights a torch and lays it behind the altar, a flickering glow will illuminate the rays – a true Sun God, yes?'

Janus had nodded, sinking deeper into the hot water. 'And will that make the Sun God look upon us fondly, my friend? It is far too dreary in this place. I do believe Mithras has been avoiding us.' He plunged his head beneath the water and emerged, shaking his hair out like a dog. The water laid it sleek against his skull, glistening the blue-black of a raven's wing.

'Ah, Janus my friend. Do not be disheartened. We have much to look forward to at this outpost. We have been promised a celebration for Saturnalia; and shortly after that, our new Commander will be taking up residence.'

Janus glowered.'I have heard a rumour that he is a Christian,' he said, placing his hands on the edge of the bath. He raised himself out of the pool and stood on the side looking down at Marcus. Rivulets of water dripped down his body, making channels between the well-defined muscles on his chest.

'A Christian?' laughed Marcus. 'I do believe our god Mithras, along with the goddess Coventina and the sacred water nymphs will defy him in some way then. This land is dedicated to them. A Christian is no match for our deities.'

'Yes. It is a pity they say the ordeal pit in our temple is no longer in use. I feel our brothers in the cult may have been able to convert him back, given the opportunity.'

'Maybe,' smiled Marcus. 'Yet the rumours could be unfounded. If that is not so, then I hope he does not appear before the Saturnalia celebration. That would be an ordeal I am not willing to go through with.'

'Ah, so Lucius was speaking the truth when he suggested you would favour dressing as a woman for this celebration?'

'It is tradition, my dear Janus. Men dress as women, masters as servants. The ordinary rules of life are turned upside down.'

'But, my friend, there is no rule to say you have to enjoy it quite so much as you appear to do,' said Janus. Laughing, he turned and made his way back towards the dressing room, Marcus' protestations lost in the echoes of the other conversations in the bath house.

# 2010

The two teenagers stepped off the bus and looked around at the rolling green hills, which stretched across the countryside towards Hexham. The car park at Brocolitia was practically empty; there was just a small van which seemed to sell drinks situated next to the pay and display machine and a camper van which was parked in the top corner. Some family had set out a picnic table between the van and the wall, but it seemed as if they had deserted it in favour of a trek across the countryside.

'Where's this temple, then?' asked Ryan.

'Down there – through those fields,' said Liv. 'It's dedicated to Mithras. I think they found it in 1949 or something.' She shuffled her papers around and studied them. It was a warm day and she had a sticky, sweaty face. Her sunglasses slid down towards the end of her nose as she flicked through the pages of printouts. The internet was a marvellous resource, even if she had managed to bring too much information and had difficulty stuffing everything into her rucksack for the day trip. 'It says here that they also had a Shrine to the Water Nymphs, and a Sacred Well, dedicated to the goddess Coventina. It's the spring where Meggie's Dene Burn starts. Legend has it, that they threw a witch's ashes into the stream, which is how it got its name. Oh look – that must be the fort there. Carrawburgh.'

Liv wandered over to a stile, which invited tourists to clamber over it and explore the site of Carrawburgh Fort. There wasn't much to see, just a huge, green mound and a few rocks sticking out of the ground.

'I think it's really sad,' said Liv. 'Imagine all those people who lived and worked here. It got destroyed somewhere around the fourth century and then a chap called Clayton dug it up again in the 1800's.' She flicked through the papers again. 'Yes. He found a military bath house in 1873, over there, I think.' She gestured to the west. 'And in1876 he discovered the "south-west interval tower of the fort itself." Are you listening, Ryan? This is really interesting.'

Ryan shuddered. 'A witch. Marvellous. You lost me at "witch". Jeez, this place gives me the creeps.' He looked around him, a hunted expression on his face as if some wild woman with warts and a broomstick was going to fly out of nowhere and attack him.

'Don't be so pathetic,' snapped Liv. 'Come on. Let's have a look around.' She scrambled over the stile and stood on the grassy mound which had been Carrawburgh fort. 'It's such a shame there's nothing left here,' she said. 'You can feel it buzzing with energy, can't you?' Luckily, she didn't wait for a response because Ryan wasn't going to give one. He didn't understand Liv's obsession with the Romans. As far as he was concerned, he'd abandoned them in year nine when he'd opted out of a GCSE in history. Liv, however, had done the whole thing. An 'A*' at GCSE and now a predicted 'A' at A-level. She was even talking about studying history at University. He sauntered up to where Liv was standing, looking out over the B6318 road. She raised her mobile phone up and took a picture. The 'click' sounded incongruous against the silence of the countryside. It seemed as if there was nobody around them for miles.

'It's supposed to be a really spiritual area around here,' Liv said. 'I need to see it for my project. Come on.' She started off across the fort. 'Look!' She walked right up to the perimeter of the grassy mound and placed her toes squarely on the edge of it. A sheer drop reminded her she was standing on an ancient monument, built on a hillside. 'There's the temple.' She indicated a grey, rectangular structure, about five blocks of stone high, in the valley below her.

'Mmm,' said Ryan wandering over to join her. 'Not much of it left, is there? Ouch!' He leaned down to rub his leg as a stray nettle attacked him. 'They could clear this place up a bit, couldn't they?'

Liv sighed and pushed her sunglasses up onto the top of her head. 'Yes, it would be great if they could re-excavate it, but I guess it's just not practical. The Shrine to the Water Nymphs was just next to the temple. There's nothing left of that either, though. I think the altars they found are at Chesters museum. We could go there after this?' she said hopefully. 'I was reading up on the inscriptions before – someone dedicated an altar to the "Nymphs and the Genius of this place." The soldiers were from Holland and Germany you know. The First Cohort of Batavians. Some of the bravest soldiers in the empire. They are the ones who introduced Mithraism here and built that temple.'

'Enough of the history lesson, Liv!' howled Ryan in mock despair. 'I know you're all excited but it means nothing to me!' Liv stuck her tongue out at him and walked away, further along the perimeter.

'Coventina's Well,' she muttered. She squinted into the sunlight, narrowing her eyes against the brightness. 'Should be about...there. Of course. That must be it.'

Ryan followed her gaze and shaded his eyes with his hands. 'A pond,' he stated. 'Nothing but a muddy pond.'

Liv shook her head. 'No, you're looking in the wrong place. It's there – that square bit with the wall around it. See? There's someone looking at it.'

'Nope. Just a pond,' repeated Ryan. 'Seriously. A pond. With about two metres of mud surrounding it.'

Liv pulled her sunglasses down onto her nose and stared out again. 'Oh! Yes. You're right. It's the sun in my eyes! Again, what a shame. The history of that place...'

'Olivia!'

'Sorry!' she said, laughing.

# 1650

'Meggie!' a voice hissed from the gap between two cottages. Meggie turned, unsure of the voice's owner. A few villagers were suspicious of her gifts; some were openly mocking, yet others, maybe even this person, wanted to believe and wanted her help. But they didn't always want other people to know.

'Hello?' she called. 'Who's there?'

'It is I, Charles Hay,' replied the voice. Meggie closed her eyes briefly and her heart sank. Charles Hay; a young man so privileged and spoiled, that he swaggered around believing he only had to ask for something and it would be his. Meggie had been summoned by him or his father on more than one occasion.

'Mr Hay, sir,' she said, moving towards the alleyway. 'And how are you today?' She didn't really care how he was. In her mind, he could be writhing in agony from a fever and she wouldn't hurry to bring him a tincture to cure him. Charles moved closer to her so his face was half in the sunlight and he smiled. His fair, wavy hair was pulled back loosely and tied with a blue velvet ribbon. Charles was, at twenty, only a year or so older than Meggie; but at times he acted like a petulant child. At others, he acted like a man of the world. Today, he seemed relaxed and cheerful, leaning against a wall and tapping a riding whip against his thigh.

'I'm extraordinarily well, thank you,' he replied. He pushed himself off the wall and stood facing the girl. In one seamless movement, he brought out his arm and pulled Meggie into the alleyway. He pushed her against the wall and planted one hand either side of her head. Meggie could smell some sort of lavender perfume emanating from his crisp, white shirt and pressed riding breeches. It made her horribly conscious of how she must look and smell to him at such close quarters. 'Ah Meggie. You are glorious. And so pretty. I'd never noticed before.' He laughed as Meggie blushed and turned her face away from him. She pressed herself backwards into the wall, feeling the cold stone through her shabby dress. Then he pushed himself away from the wall and stood looking down at her, smirking.

'It worked then,' she stated. Charles nodded.

'It did indeed. Thank you. Once again. Now would you please just call in on the poor girl and make sure she isn't suffering any ill effects. I would be most grateful.'

Meggie nodded mutely. How many children would Charles Hay have spawned by now if Meggie had not been called upon to intervene? She hated it. But what option did she have? She hated to see a pathetically grateful village girl kneeling before her and crying with relief. That was worse, in a way, than being asked to deal with the problem in the first place.

'Tell me, Meggie,' asked Hay curiously. 'What is it that you give them?'

Meggie shook her head. She would not share her secrets with him. The mugwort she used was dangerous if you miscalculatcd the dosage. Picked at midnight, on the Summer Solstice, it had never failed Meggie yet.

'What does it matter to you, Mr Hay?' she asked. 'So long as it does its job.'

Hay sighed.'You are right, my dear Miss Meg,' he said. 'Later. I'll send someone with the payment later.'

'Thank you, Mr Hay,' she said.

'No. Thank you,' he replied. He bent his head down and kissed her on the cheek. Meggie fought the urge to cringe. She didn't want him to see how scared she was of him. Hay laughed, and turned on his heel. He headed back down the alley whistling to himself, tapping the shaft of his whip in tune.

Meggie watched him go, then she sent a quick prayer to Mother Earth and Brigantia, the ancient fertility goddess. She made a mental note to offer something back to them, in exchange for the life she had taken from them.

# AD 390

Marcus lay naked and blindfolded on the floor of the temple. His face was pressed against the stone flags, his arms and legs were spreadeagled as he emulated the rays of the Sun God. The Pater raised his staff and intoned the words of initiation.

'As the sun spirals its longest dance, cleanse your servant. As nature shows bounty and fertility, bless your servant. Let your servant live with the true intent of Mithras and enable him to fulfil his destiny. Marcus Simplicius Simplex, arise from the rock as our god Mithras was born from the rock. Let us witness the Water Miracle.'

Marcus raised himself up, his limbs stiff and sore from the position he had been forced to assume for so long. He stumbled as he stood up, disorientated by the low chanting which filled the temple. He felt two men grasp his wrists and roughly bind them together, so they were fettered before him.

'The Heliodromus, my Sun Runners, have bound you with their whips,' said the Pater. 'You must take this lance from my soldiers and strike the stone before you, releasing water from the stone as Mithras released it.'

Marcus felt the wooden shaft of a spear be forced into his clasped hands. He knew that the Miles, or the Soldiers of Mithras, were the third ranking up in the cult. Today, Marcus hoped to become a Corax; a Raven. This was the first level and equated with the protection of Mercury. He shifted the spear so he had a better grip on it and squared his feet. The chanting was becoming louder. He felt his heart banging against his chest. He was a soldier of the First Batavian Cohort. He could do this. The chanting reached a crescendo, and he yelled out as he charged blindly forward.

Marcus felt the point of the spear strike something hard. There was a crack and a crumbling sound and he pitched forward, the object giving way as the lance dug into it. He fell to his knees. There was a gushing sound as water burst forth from something and soaked him. He threw the spear down and the chanting stopped abruptly.

'Marcus Simplicius Simplex. You have released water from the rock. We shall not sacrifice today – the Corax does not sacrifice. Instead, let us feast as Mithras feasted on the bull, and bow down to our god.'

Someone ripped the blindfold off him and Marcus blinked as his eyes became accustomed to the darkness in the temple. There were no windows in these temples to Mithras, no light except that of candlelight. He found he was staring at the shattered remains of a clay vessel, which still dripped with water. Shadows flickered weirdly across it, and a cult member appeared soundlessly beside him and swept the pieces of the vessel away. Several men were ranged around the altar area where Marcus knelt. They stood silently, arms behind their backs, their faces covered with masks. There was no way of knowing who was behind the masks and Marcus suppressed a shudder. Although he worked with these men daily, the cult decreed secrecy and until he rose through the ranks, he would remain ignorant of the soldiers who carried out the rituals.

The Pater, or Father, of the cult was the highest ranking member there. He wore a head-dress that mirrored the rays of the sun and extended down to cover his face. He was wearing vibrantly coloured robes of ruby red and citrine yellow and was carrying a staff decorated with flowing ribbons of red and yellow material. Marcus stared up at him in awe. The Pater was reclining on a stone plinth, watching him.

'I submit to you, Pater, as Sol submitted to Mithras,' whispered Marcus and bowed his head to the Pater.

'Welcome, Corax Marcus,' said the Pater. 'Arise and be clothed in deference to our god.' Marcus stood up and another man brought a simple sacking loin cloth over to him. Marcus allowed the man to dress him and bowed once more to the Pater.

The Pater held his hand out to Marcus. 'Let us shake hands as Mithras shook hands with Sol,' he said. 'We are now united with a handshake. You are welcomed, not only as a Corax, but as a syndexioi; an initiate.'

'Thank you, Pater. I shall carry out my duty as you decree,' he said.

'You shall, Corax Marcus. It is part of our cult,' said the Pater.

Marcus knew that he was serious.

# 2010

Liv clambered back over the stile and adjusted her backpack. 'This way now, Ryan,' she called. 'We have to go down this path and through the field. If we skirt around the edge of the fort, we'll get to the temple. Ooh. I wonder where the cemetery was...it was...' she referred to her notes again. 'It was..west. Again. West of here. They found some tombstones in the bath house, you know. Trumpeters and standard bearers. Trumpeters were held in really high regard. They were exempt from the normal soldier duties, you know. And standard bearers. Well! Talk about the best men in the legion...'

Ryan thought it was best not to answer her or encourage her in any way. That way, she couldn't strike up a conversation about any sort of Roman remains – be them bodily remains or shrine-like remains or fort-like remains. He kind of thought that he might be a little bit in love with Liv; but at times like this, he wondered whether they actually had any basis whatsoever for a long-term relationship. He imagined conversations about history around the dinner table, or Liv taking off for months on end to dig around some old Roman ruin they had hardly discovered yet. Archaeology. That was another thing she was banging on about. She fancied archaeology as well as history at Uni. Would it work? He didn't know. He was glad in some ways that he hadn't pushed the subject of a relationship with her, just in case.

'There are cows here,' he muttered. 'And sheep. Look. Living things. There's crap everywhere. Why are we heading through a field of crap?'

Liv was stomping ahead, throwing facts and figures over her shoulder at Ryan. He sent up a small prayer of thanks to whichever gods were listening, that the history lesson was getting whipped away by the summer breeze.

'Shall we do the Well first or the temple?' Liv called out.

'Does my opinion really matter?' moaned Ryan.

'No, not really,' replied Liv. 'So let's do...the Well.' She circumvented the temple area and began to march across the field, following a pathway made of flattened, dried grass. She didn't really know where she was going; but, and she couldn't explain this to Ryan for fear of him thinking she was completely crazy, she felt a strange sort of pull to Coventina's Well. She didn't know why. But she knew she wanted to go there.

# AD 390

'Janus! Janus! Are you able to speak with me?' hissed Marcus, as they passed one another on the main pathway through the vicus. Janus knew of a very good gambling house in the township, or the vicus, which had sprung up around Carrawburgh fort, and he often spent his evenings throwing dice with the men who ran it. It was next door to a house where a beautiful sloe-eyed girl lived with five of her 'sisters'; and it was not unknown for the soldiers to visit these ladies for a little conversation and comfort. The auxiliary soldiers were unable to marry – but when they were discharged from the army, their uxorio – or co-habitation – could then became a legal marriage. Until then, they kept their 'wives' and children close by in the townships near their forts. As well as an assortment of families relating to the Batavian Cohort, the vicus near Carrawburgh housed at least three places of worship; the Mithraic Temple, the Shrine of the Water Nymphs and Coventina's Well. The bubbles of excitement kept rising up in his stomach, and Marcus was finding it increasingly difficult to keep his initiation secret. Surely, it would do no harm to tell Janus?

Marcus ducked out of the way as a cart carrying animals ready for slaughter bounced along the rutted road and called out to get Janus' attention again.

'Marcus! My friend! What is this urgency?' laughed Janus. He was in a good mood, his gambling for once having a positive effect on his fortunes.

'I need to speak to you. I have something to tell you,' said Marcus. Janus could tell that he was fizzing with energy.

'I see this is important to you,' Janus said. 'Let us take some wine together at this establishment and you can tell me. It is obvious you are delighted about something. Or someone. Tell me; what is her name?'

Marcus laughed. Women, for all they were marvellous creatures, were way down on his list of priorities at the minute. He was a Corax! He had been accepted and initiated into the cult of Mithras. What more could he want from life at this moment in time?

The two men ducked into the public house and Janus ordered a flagon of wine.

'Janus, I feel ashamed that you are purchasing this wine for us when I am the one who has need to celebrate!' cried Marcus, throwing himself onto a bench in the corner of the room. Janus waved his hand.

'No, it is my pleasure, dear friend. I have been lucky tonight- The goddess Fortuna has smiled upon me. Now. What is it you need to tell me?'

'I have been accepted as a Corax into the cult of Mitrhras!' said Marcus. 'A Raven. The very first step on the ladder!'

'No!' cried Janus. 'That is worthy of a celebration indeed, my friend!' He leaned over to Marcus. 'Do you realise how fortunate you are? It is every man's dream to become initiated into the cult of Mithras. Tell me; what ordeal did you have to perform for them? Or do you no longer call them ordeals? Now that there is allegedly no ordeal pit.'

Janus shook his head, but failed to stop the grin spreading across his face.

'I cannot tell you,' he said. 'It is a secret ceremony. And only those lucky enough to be accepted into the Cult can discuss it.'

'Ah, Marcus! We are good friends! Why do you not tell me the whole story?' cried Janus, refilling Marcus' glass. 'Please. I shall not divulge it. You can tell me, your oldest friend!' His dark eyes twinkled with mischief and his handsome face creased into a grin. 'Please. You know you want to!'

'I know I want to!' laughed Marcus. 'But I am afraid I cannot tell you.'

'No! You cannot tell me half a story!' moaned Janus, rolling his eyes and clasping his hand to his forehead. 'What if I want to do it? Who shall advise me if you, my dearest friend, will not do so?'

'You shall simply have to join the cult, as I did,' said Marcus. 'The Pater will advise you on what you need to do. He is the man with the power. He is the man who walks with Mithras.'

Janus nodded slowly. 'I see. We know the temple is there. But the rites are secretive.' He shook his head. 'However. It is maybe something I will consider in the future. After the new Commandant arrives. The stronger our support for our ancient deities the better. The more power we have over these Christians that force us to change our beliefs, the better. Shall we drink to that, my friend?' Janus raised his glass to Marcus and took a deep swig from it. Marcus echoed the action

'Indeed, my friend,' he said seriously. 'Let us drink to Mithras and our sacred deities. And let no Christians tear us asunder.'

# 1650

A gaggle of village women stood by the edge of the market, arms folded and baskets laden with purchases. Some of their items had been paid for, others had been bartered for. Stray chickens and animals wandered amongst the merchants and bits of old straw and rubbish littered the ground.

'If I was her, I'd watch my step,' said one of them. 'I heard tell there's a man been to Newcastle who's flushed them all out over there.' The rest of the women nodded in agreement.

'The likes of her should be careful,' muttered another - a toothless old biddy who walked with a stoop and stank of ale.

'You're just worried about yourself,' said another one snidely. 'You can see the signs on any old woman if you know what to look for. They just need to see you and they can tell. Then they do the test and that proves it.'

Meggie hurried past the women, her head down and her shawl pulled over her hair. In another life, Meggie would have been beautiful. Her hair would have been ash blonde and her eyes a soft, dove grey. Her skin would have been smooth and peachy and her smile would have lit up her oval face. Living in this village, however, the reality was different. Her hair, although blonde, would hang in greasy rats' tails over her shoulders until she managed to wash it with some rough soap and a pail of water. Her grey eyes were haunted and as she was short-sighted, she squinted, which had the effect of creasing her face into a scowl as she studied distant objects. Her face was too gaunt to be smooth; instead her cheekbones were planed and angular and her eyes appeared too big. The worst thing was, Meggie knew all of this. She knew that she could have been beautiful if she had been given the privileges Charles Hay had. She knew he mocked her when he told her she was pretty. But, on the other hand, she had much to be grateful for. If she was truly beautiful, like some of the village girls, then she could have been in the same situation as they had been, when she had been ordered to help them out of it. Charles Hay would not just tease her, but he would target her. And what she lacked in beauty, she made up for in knowledge – the knowledge she had gleaned from the world around her and the ancient tales her Grandmother had told her. Meggie was an autumn-child. Her Grandmother told her she had given her hazelnut milk to drink when she was a baby, in order to encourage her abilities.

'Yes,' said the first gossip, watching Meggie scurry by, 'she ought to watch herself, that one.'

'But didn't she sort you out, when you had that foul rash last year?' asked the snide one. The first woman flushed an ugly red.

'That's as may be,' she said. 'But it's still unnatural what she does. It just needs to go bad the once, and she'll be in trouble.'

Meggie was oblivious to all this. She needed to go to the Sacred Well – the meeting with Charles Hay had unsettled her, and only by distancing herself from the village, could she find any sort of inner peace.

# 2010

Liv walked along the grassy path across the field and scanned the area ahead of her for any sign of Coventina's Well. She was fairly sure it was along here. Looking down on it from Carrawburgh had played havoc with her perspective, throwing her geography into disarray as well as throwing a mirage at her.

She looked down at her notes and stopped where the grassy path led off on a smaller track, obviously well used by sheep, cows and other farming stock. It was narrow and straight, heading directly towards a muddy mess by the fence. Tall, white flowers, like stars, nodded towards the mud, and delicate fronds of greenery dripping with more pale flowers fluffed around the edges of a grey, marshy pool.

'That's it,' said Liv. 'That's the Well.' She looked around for Ryan. He had wandered off up the hill, away from the Well, for some reason. She opened her mouth to call him down, but then thought better of it. It didn't seem right to shout or to raise voices here. It was strangely peaceful. Liv felt calm and tranquil, standing at this sacred spring, which burst through the moorland and fed the burn, running into the River South Tyne near Stanegate fort at Newbrough, three miles south. She looked up at Carrawburgh and tried to imagine it when it was inhabited by the Batavian Cohort. It would have been immense – soldiers moving briskly around, planning battles, perhaps, or just looking after the day to day arrangements of the fort. Someone was up there now – maybe a backpacker, or one of the holidaymakers from the camper van. She could see them standing on the edge, looking down towards the Mithraeum. Then they turned and moved away, disappearing behind a scrubby bush, no doubt on their way back to the car park. Liv heard footsteps as Ryan came up behind her. He put his hand on her shoulder and she turned to speak to him.

But her heart skipped a beat when she realised that Ryan was still on the hillside, staring out across the fields. And she was still alone, next to an ancient sacred spring in the shadow of a ruined fort.

# AD 390

'Io, Saturnalia!' cried Janus. He was dressed in women's clothing and had a wreath of ivy and berries balanced on his head. Ridiculous as he should have looked, Marcus was forced to admit he carried it off well. Janus was tall and muscular; olive-skinned and dark-haired, he was one of the few true Romans in the cohort. He seemed to have been born with confidence and a natural ability to lead. He was the unanimous choice for the Saturnalicius princeps, and as such would lead the Saturnalia celebrations. Other members of the cohort, like Marcus, had come from Germania Inferior; the area that would eventually become known as the Netherlands. They were happy to be guided by Janus this year – nobody knew how the new Commandant would react to future celebrations if the rumours were true, so they were determined to enjoy themselves while they could.

'Ho! Praise to Saturn!' laughed Marcus in response. He was wearing a colourful outfit begged from one of the sloe-eyed sisters in the vicus. As he left her house, Aelia had placed the pileus, or 'freedman's hat' on his fair hair and stretched up to kiss him.

'Enjoy yourself this week. It is the strangest sight, seeing all you men dressed as women,' she said. 'I hope you do not forget yourselves and become less than masculine after the celebrations end!'

'With beauties such as you and your sisters so close to us, that is hardly likely!' said Marcus. 'Thank you once again for these wonderful robes!' He lifted the edge of the purple cloth and let it drop again. 'I cannot recall seeing you in this, Aelia? I hope it is not your best outfit. I cannot forgive myself if that is so.'

'Dear Marcus! Do not worry. I have many, many outfits. You beautiful men do not see most of them! Or indeed, do you even see any of them?' Her eyes twinkled and she kissed him again. 'Just return my dress after the week is over and do not forget who you are. Agreed?'

'Agreed,' said Marcus. He bowed to her and made his way back to the fort. On his way, he threw a few coins into the Sacred Well. The cohort had dedicated this Well to Coventina, the water goddess. It was an open air shrine, made from a natural spring which started at the Well and gurgled past the Mithraeum and the shrine to the Water Nymphs. One day, he had walked the length of the stream and stood and watched as it emptied into the River Tinea, near Carvoran fort. He had a great respect for Coventina. She was the goddess who eased them out of the harsh winters they experienced at Carrawburgh; the goddess who helped the ice and snow melt and returned water to the frozen landscape. This Saturnalia, her help would be appreciated more than usual. The ground was icy underfoot and drifts of snow piled up against the walls of the fort and the buildings in the vicus. Someone had been out and broken the thick ice which had formed on the surface of the Well. Marcus thought it would do no harm to pacify Coventina by offering her a few denarii. What did the coins matter to him, really, anyway? He was well-paid and could afford to give some coins to the goddess.

Marcus walked past the Mithraeum, and stole a glance inside it. The door was open, which was unusual. He could see someone inside, reaching their hand out to touch an altar; another soldier, he guessed, celebrating Saturnalia by being clothed in white. His heart swelled with pride as he thought about his altar, which now stood propped up against the inside wall.

DEO INVICTO MITRAE M SIMPLICIVS SIMPLEX PREF VSLM

"To the Invincible God Mithras, the prefect Marcus Simplicius Simplex, willingly and deservedly fulfills his vow."

He knew this would be the case, whatever the Pater asked him to do. Being initiated into the cult was the second most important thing he had done in his life. The first thing, had been to join the Roman Army.

Marcus had walked on past the temple and up to the fort. He nodded at the guard standing at the gate, and the guard moved aside to let Marcus in. It looked faintly ludicrous – both the men wore female clothing and hats, yet they still had the stature and bearing of soldiers. Saturnalia was a time for revelry and feasting; a time to eat, drink and be merry. The fort was decorated in swathes of greenery and candles stood in alcoves and niches around the building. A long, low couch had been placed in the quadrant inside the fort, and it was on this that Janus was reclining.

Two of the most honoured officers in the Cohort stood to his side, and he waved them away regally as Marcus approached him. 'Please, bring my friend Marcus some wine and some food. He must be tired after his exercise,' called Janus. The men bowed and moved away from the couch. Janus grinned at Marcus. 'I do so love it when we are able to order the likes of Longinius and Milenius around. Buglers and standard-bearers – pah! They think they are as godly as Saturn himself. It is a shame that we can only do this for seven days.' He sighed theatrically, and beckoned Marcus over to him. 'So.' He lowered his voice. 'Whilst my slaves are otherwise engaged, let me discuss some interesting information with you. Not only does our new Commandant seemingly worship the Christian God, but he is a firm follower of the Emperor.'

'No!' cried Marcus, opening his eyes wide. 'So all this...' he gestured around the fort. 'All the celebrations will be stopped once he comes? And that is definite?'

Janus nodded. 'I am afraid it seems that will be the case. Theodosius' people have already been despatched to break up certain temples. It is he we must thank for criminalising our sacrifices. We might be fortunate and maintain some of our Saturnalia celebrations, as it co-incides with the Christian Yuletide celebrations. But I fear for our shrines and our Mithraeum once he arrives.' Janus pulled a face. 'I can only hope that the information is incorrect on some level. For the likes of you, this will make your next step up the Mithraic ladder seem further away than ever. It seemed as if you had your name down for months, before your initiation as a Corax.' His face fell. 'I suppose it is no good me putting my name forward to follow you, if this is going to happen. I might as well go back to Rome and throw myself to the lions if I will be forced to become a Christian.'

'I don't know what to say,' whispered Marcus. 'It is wrong. We have been sent to this outpost, forced to retreat from Caledonia and now we have to bow to this man. It is all wrong.' He balled his fist and punched it off his thigh. 'Janus, let me speak to the Pater. He may be able to initiate you as a favour to me, if I tell him this news...'

'No!' hissed Janus looking worried. 'You can't tell him the information came from me. He might think that I used to my advantage, to ensure I was initiated. Please. Do not mention it to anyone. Just – just take my name to him and let him know I am interested. At least I will be on record. And if all this comes to nothing, I may eventually be able to worship inside the temple with you.' He smiled at Marcus, and clapped him on the shoulder. 'Would you do that for me?'

Marcus nodded. 'Certainly, my friend. I shall let it be known you are interested. And if our god wills it, you shall be initiated as a Corax and we shall work together in the service of Mithras.'

'Thank you,' said Janus. 'I appreciate it. I shall offer something to Coventina and the water nymphs next time I am passing. It cannot do any harm to have them on my side, can it?'

'Not at all,' replied Marcus. He looked up. The two officers were coming back with glasses of wine and a plate of food. They looked preposterous, dressed up as women and doing the work of a slave; Marcus couldn't help but laugh at them.

'Thank you my dear slaves,' he called. 'I shall recommend you to your master.'

Milenius, a standard-bearer and therefore a highly privileged man in the cohort laughed good-naturedly. 'Enjoy it, Marcus Simplicius Simplex. I shall store all this up here,' he tapped his head with his forefinger, 'and remember it. Six more days, my friend. Only six more days!'

'Ah, and what a wonderful six days it shall be,' retorted Marcus taking a glass and raising it to Milenius. He took a sip and rolled the wine around his mouth, tasting the rich berries. 'Is this your best wine, Slave? If I find you are giving me the dregs from your amphoras, I shall be forced to make a complaint to your master.'

'Only the best for you, Sir,' said Milenius and bowed low. 'Would I ever give you bad wine?'

'Am I able to trust you, then?' asked Marcus, taking another sip of wine.

'For six more days you can,' replied Milenius, barely hiding his smile. 'For six more days. Then I shall tell everyone how much you enjoy dressing as a woman. Lucius was right.'

One evening later that week, Marcus slipped into the Mithraic Temple. He had discarded his women's clothing and dressed in his Corax loincloth, wrapping a thick woollen blanket around his body. It was bitterly cold, with a fresh snowfall and a whirling blizzard covering the countryside. He was shivering as he took his place on the feasting benches, next to the statue of Cautopates. Plenty of candles had been lit and the temple was filled with a smoky haze, but it did not do much to disguise the fact that it was bleakest winter outside. The stone plinth was covered with animal skins and the Nymphus were walking down the aisle holding their lamps before them. The other grades of initiate were processing behind them, amongst them, the Leos, carrying carved thunderbolts before them, and the Perses, who held images of the moon and stars aloft.

Marcus joined in with the chanting as the procession passed him. The Pater was at the back, flanked again by his Miles, or soldiers. He took his place on the stone plinth and began the ceremony. Marcus participated whole-heartedly, despite the coldness of the cave-like building, and privately wondered when it would be the best time to approach the Pater about Janus.

At the end of the ceremony, the cult members partook of a feast. Marcus raised his glass along with the others, and wryly considered how much wine he had consumed over the past few days. He knew the major ceremony for Mithras was at mid-summer, to celebrate the solstice. Marcus had wondered whether they would still be worshipping Mithras by mid-summer, knowing what he now knew about the Commandant. All the more reason to approach the Pater about Janus as soon as possible.

Marcus got up from his seat with the other cult members and wandered around the temple, chatting to people. As a Corax, he was the only level of initiate not to wear a mask. As such, there was only one Corax at a time. This was to preserve the mystery of the higher echelons and to remind the Corax that they were the lowest of the low. That was why their identity was not hidden within the temple walls. It felt odd talking to people who you did not recognize. He had his suspicions about the odd person here and there; a movement, a gesture familiar to them, and he could sometimes make an educated guess. He felt certain that one of the Leos was Lucius; he had a particular way of standing. An old wound had left him putting more weight on his left leg than was usual. The Leo in question seemed as if he tried to compensate for this, and as such looked awkward and ill at ease. Which was why, Marcus noticed, he sat down more than the other Leos.

Marcus took a deep breath and approached the man he thought was Lucius. 'May I ask your advice, Sir?' he began. The man turned his head towards Marcus and nodded.

THE MEMORY OF SNOW

'You may, Corax,' he replied. His voice was muffled through the head-dress. Marcus had realised, to his mild annoyance, a while ago, that you could not even identify the members from their voices.

'I have a friend who is interested in joining our cult. I need to pass his name on to the Pater. How do you suggest I do this?'

'Why can he not go through the correct channels?' asked the Leo. 'His name shall stay on the list until the Pater decides and works through it.'

'It's...complicated,' said Marcus. He felt his cheeks redden, despite the chill in the air. How could he explain his reasoning to the Leo? 'Perhaps I should just ask the Pater directly. Do you think he would accept it?'

The Leo laughed. 'You have much to learn, Corax,' he said. 'We do not bother the Pater with such requests. If you are desperate, you could try to speak to his Heliodromus. As we are celebrating Saturnalia outside in the fort, the hierarchy may be slightly more open to your suggestions. After all, doesn't our Pater fall under the protection of Saturn? As second-in-command, the Heliodromus could attempt to grant you an audience, if the Pater accepts it.'

'Thank you. I shall do that,' replied Marcus. 'I realise that you act in my best interests here, Sir. You cannot bring pain or harm or anything impure to bear at your grade. Which is why I requested your counsel in the first place. I thank you once again.' He inclined his head and moved away from the Leo. He looked around the temple and caught sight of a Heliodromus. He had no idea who these men were – so he would act in deference to them, as befitted his status in the cult, and beg them for an audience from the Pater.

Ten minutes later, Marcus found himself escorted to a screened off portion of the temple. His heart was banging against his chest and his palms were horribly sweaty. Which was ridiculous, because he obviously worked with the man he was about to see. He just didn't know who he was. And here in the temple, normal day-to-day relationships in the fort did not count.

'I have been advised that you wish to speak with me privately?' said the Pater.

'Yes Sir,' replied Marcus, kneeling before him. 'I was hoping you could advise me about something.'

'Go ahead, Corax,' said the Pater. 'I am listening.'

Marcus took a deep breath.'I have a good friend who wishes to join our worship of Mithras,' he said. 'He would like to be considered for an initiation into the cult.'

'So he must go through the correct channels. As you did. Then I shall discuss his case with my colleagues and add him to the waiting list. Is that all?' said the Pater, looking down at Marcus.

'No – it's…complicated. I don't know if we have much…time to do this. He was wondering…' Marcus tailed off, suddenly deflated. It was hopeless. He would have to tell Janus tomorrow he had been unsuccessful. It was ridiculous to even think that he could have pushed his friend up the waiting list, even if there was no threat of a Christian Commandant coming to Carrawburgh. 'I'm sorry. It was stupid of me. Forgive me,' he said, bowing. 'I will advise him of the correct procedures and he shall have to adhere to them.'

'Hmm,' said the Pater. 'You have me slightly intrigued now. You say there is an urgency to this. Your friend is unwilling to wait for a place, and is desperate to become part of us. Is that correct?'

'Yes, Pater,' replied Marcus.

'I wonder – is he perhaps due a posting?' said the Pater. 'Good luck to him if he is. I sincerely hope he finds himself somewhere warmer than here. Or could it be something else? I have heard a nasty rumour, Corax. Regarding our new Commandant. Could it have something to do with him?'

Marcus did not reply. He felt himself blush. Janus had sworn him to secrecy, yet the rumour mills had already began to grind.

'I cannot say, Sir,' Marcus said finally. 'All I can say, is that, as far as I am aware, he is not due a posting elsewhere.'

'Leave his name with my Heliodromus,' said the Pater. 'I shall not promise anything, but I shall consider what you have told me. Or what you have not told me. This is quite an interesting development. I hope it shall not have a detrimental effect on our worship; both here and at the shrines nearby. Thank you, Corax. I have enjoyed our little chat this evening. Blessings of Mithras be upon you. I shall be curious to watch how this develops.'

'Thank you, Pater,' murmured Marcus. 'I appreciate all you have done for me. If there is anything I can do...'

The Pater raised his hand, silencing Marcus.'Thank you, Corax. I shall bear that in mind for the future. For now, just live by the ethos of Mithras and fulfill your vow as one of his worshippers.'

'Your will and Mithras' will shall be done,' said Marcus. 'I now take my leave of you, Pater, and thank you once more from the bottom of my heart.'

Marcus backed out of the room, and was escorted back into the feast by the Heliodromus who had taken him to see the Pater.'Janus. My friend is Janus Cosconianus,' he said to the sunrunner. The man simply nodded at him, and disappeared into the throng

# 2010

Liv was sure she had felt someone touch her shoulder. She shivered and looked around her. Ryan was way up on the hillside, jiggling from foot to foot. He had been moaning that his feet were sore this morning, barely even before they left home. Liv opened her mouth to call him, but again had the feeling that she mustn't raise her voice here. The Sacred Well had to remain a place of calmness and peace. She looked up at the fort and scanned the horizon for the man she had seen on the top. He had disappeared as well.

She realised she was beginning to sink into the mud and stepped away from the Well, onto firmer grass.

'You had enough, then?' called Ryan from his position on the hillside. He obviously didn't feel the need to remain quiet in this place.

'Did anybody pass you?' asked Liv, knowing the answer already. 'Just before. When I was down here?'

'Nope. Nobody here except us,' replied Ryan. He turned and half-walked, half-skidded down the dry hillside to join her. The summer grass up on the hill was quite a contrast to the thick mud which seeped out of Coventina's Well. 'Haven't seen anyone around here at all. Why? Do you think some other mad people are going to be wandering around an old puddle and a pile of old stones? I mean, come on. The Roman's have had, what, two thousand years to re-build their stuff? You'd think they would have done something about it by now.'

'You're so funny,' said Liv. She was sharper than she meant to be with him. She felt a little unsettled and couldn't resist having another look around her. She saw someone pass by the entrance to the temple and pointed. 'Look. There's someone else 'mad enough' to be here. Do you want to go and tell her you think she's mad?'

'Well, maybe she isn't mad,' said Ryan, watching a middle-aged woman with frizzy hair and a backpack enter the temple from the opposite hillside. 'She's all togged up for it, anyway. She probably meant to come here. She's probably doing that Hadrian's Walk thing. I just meant that we were a bit mad. Coming to see a puddle. Well, OK, it's a special puddle. It's Coventina's Puddle. But...'

'Keep digging yourself in deeper,' growled Liv. She marched off towards the Mithraic temple, ignoring Ryan's attempts at appeasement.

Once back in the valley to the south-west of Carrawburgh, Liv began to calm down a little. She stood and looked at the Mithraic temple properly, whilst she waited for Ryan to catch her up. He'd slipped and stumbled into a hole, presumably dug by a rabbit, and was moaning about that now, instead of the other stuff.

A paved walkway led through a gap in the walls, and ended at three altars. A raised grassy area flanked the path on each side, dotted with short, stone columns. The backpacker lady was sitting on one of the raised areas, noisily unwrapping greaseproof paper from her sandwiches.

She looked up at Liv and started.'Oh! I'm sorry. I just thought I'd have my lunch here, where it's nice and quiet. I'll get out of your way, so you can see the place without any twenty-first century people spoiling it for you... I spotted you in here earlier. I thought you'd finished.'

'No, it wasn't me,' said Liv, shaking her head. 'But please. It's fine. You stay where you are. I'm waiting for him anyway,' said Liv, jerking her had behind her. Ryan was now bending over, fastening his shoelace. He had discarded his backpack and it was balanced on the edge of the hill. Liv just knew that the backpack would end up down the gully, and probably roll into Meggie's Dene Burn.

'And there it goes,' she muttered as Ryan looked in the direction of the tumbling backpack and swore loudly. He stumbled off down the bank of the stream and disappeared from view. Liv sighed. She made her way to the other side of the temple, following the wire fence that surrounded the monument. The entrance to the temple was through a kissing-gate, and she pushed it open, wincing as a loud creak echoed around the valley. She read the information board, and traced her fingers around the drawing which showed the temple in its heyday. It was difficult to equate the colourful, mystical place of fiction with the stone walls which remained in reality. It had been revealed in 1949, she read, during a long, hot summer. The water from Coventina's Well had kept the ground moist, which was why everything had been preserved. She allowed herself a little smile. The ancient gods and goddesses of the area were looking out for one another, as if they were guardians of the area. It was a shame nothing remained of the shrine to the Water Nymphs. She would have liked to have seen that as well. It was incredible what secrets the ground had kept over the centuries.

'Have you seen Coventina's Well?' asked the backpacker lady, standing up and crumpling up her sandwich wrappers. 'It's supposed to be around here somewhere.' She looked around her. 'I'm not sure where I can find it.'

'It's over there,' said Liv, indicating the area across the field. 'At least I think it is. There's a spring over there, anyway. I'd have loved to have seen it when it was in use.' The backpacker lady nodded, her curls bouncing wildly around her face.

'Me too. Such a lot of history. It's fascinating. I don't know whether I believe it was destroyed deliberately or just fell into disrepair. So many questions. I don't suppose we'll ever get the answer to them.' She shrugged. 'Some people think the offerings they found were placed there for safekeeping. Others think it was a slightly more exciting reason. Enjoy your day, anyway. I'm going to head up there and see what I can find.'

Liv smiled at the lady and stood back to let her past. Why couldn't Ryan be as excited or as interested in it? It was a Boy Thing. It had to be. And speak of the Devil; here he came, stumping up to her. He grinned at her, silently seeking absolution and hoping she was in a forgiving mood.

'So. This is the Mithraic Temple,' he said, trying to sound enthusiastic and knowledgeable. Liv nodded, looking at the backpack which was now dripping water onto the ground. Ryan had the grace to blush.

'Yes, this is the Mithraeum. This was where the Roman soldiers worshipped,' Liv said. She headed through the gap at the entrance to the temple, and walked up the central aisle to approach the altars. Ryan stood outside and looked around him. He gave a cursory glance to the information board.

'It's a bit like a sheep pen, isn't it?' he said, dumping the backpack onto the ground; where it rolled over again and settled itself in a pile of dirt.

# AD 390

Marcus had returned Aelia's purple dress to her and been thanked most delightfully for doing so. The festivities of Saturnalia were over for another year, and Marcus fingered the small bone gaming pieces Janus had given him as his token gift. He had them in a leather pouch slung around his waist, carrying them with him in case he was overcome with an urge to gamble in the vicus. As promised, Milenius had pulled rank on him for the comments he had made about his wine.

'I know you are more used to working with weapons, Marcus, but I believe my standard needs attending to. There is a small tear on the edge of it. Do you think you could mend it for me, perhaps?' Milenius had said. Marcus had taken the task on with a smile, and returned the repaired standard to his superior with good grace. Longinius had been less than forgiving with poor Janus. Janus had been tasked with polishing Longinius' bugle until it shone. Every tiny fingerprint had to be removed and the bugle had been returned to Janus three times already. Marcus found his friend mooching around the fort, his eyebrows drawn together and a dark, glowering expression on his face.

'I really do not know if it was worth being Saturnalicius princeps,' Janus grumbled, holding the bugle between thumb and forefinger distastefully. 'Remind me, if we are allowed to celebrate Saturnalia next year and I am fortunate to be elected again, to choose different slaves.'

'The choice may be slender next year,' laughed Marcus. 'You may be promoted and therefore have less superiors available to you. Or,' he shrugged, 'you could always ask the Commandant to participate,' said Marcus, his eyes sparkling with mischief.

'Merciful Jupiter!' howled Janus. 'No, please do not send that thought out into the world. I cannot imagine anything worse!'

'Then take comfort in the fact that I managed to speak to the Pater about your initiation. I cannot promise you anything, but he is willing to look at your case and decide the outcome.'

'Truly? You are a good friend, Marcus. I do not deserve you.' Janus hugged Marcus and then drew away from him, a grin splitting his face. 'Thank you. From the bottom of my heart.'

'You are most welcome, my friend,' smiled Marcus. 'As I say, he cannot promise you a quick initiation, but he is aware of your name and your interest and is willing to consider it.'

'You did not tell him anything about the new Commandant, did you?' asked Janus. 'Just…'

'No! No. I did not mention that to him,' said Marcus. He spoke the truth, although he felt uncomfortable that he had implied as much to the Pater. Still – what Janus did not know would not hurt him.

'One more thing,' said Janus, curiously. 'Who is the Pater? Do you know his identity? I am intrigued as to this secrecy that surrounds our Mithraic Temple.'

Marcus shook his head. 'I am sorry. I do not know who he is. If I did, I would go up to him and ask him to favour you directly. I somehow think that seeing his face would make me less intimidated. But I suspect his identity will remain a secret. Annoying though that is.'

Janus nodded thoughtfully. 'I agree. But still!' He smiled at Marcus and hugged him again. 'Thank you. I appreciate it. Now. I must go and polish Longinius' bugle once more.' He picked the bugle up and scowled at it. 'Do you think Coventina would accept this bugle as an offering? It would make her position stronger, no doubt. And hopefully encourage a thaw of this dreadful snow.' Janus shivered. 'How I long for a posting somewhere else in this empire,' he groaned. 'Somewhere; anywhere, where Mithras smiles upon us all and covers our world in sunlight and warmth!'

# 1650

Meggie wandered along the banks of the burn, making her way to the Sacred Well. Her Grandmother had told her that Coventina was a Roman water nymph, as well as a river goddess. The place had such a magical sense, that Meggie felt at one with the earth and the water and knew that she belonged there. Coventina had helped Meggie's people; she had melted the snow and ice and made the rivers flow again every year. Sometimes, in a long, hard winter, Meggie would make her way through snowdrifts and ice to plead with Coventina; the goddess always ended Scota, the goddess of winter's, hold and brought Spring to the countryside. Occasionally, Meggie had felt a presence at the Well. She knew it was Coventina herself, coming to bless her and keep her safe. Coventina was thankful that someone still remembered her. She would be there for Meggie, so long as Meggie did not forsake her.

Meggie had heard the women speaking in the village, and now their comments twisted around her mind like yarn on a spinning wheel. What did they mean, the man 'had flushed them out of Newcastle'? Someone had mentioned witchcraft last week in the market, and she shuddered to think about that. The dark arts. Animal sacrifice. Wishing ill on fellow human-beings. It was all so wrong. Meggie knew how to heal people and how to help people. She knew how to harness the forces of nature. She knew how to use herbs and plants to make things better. She shook her head. How could people be so unkind to others? Everything she did, was for the good of her fellow human beings. At least nobody would suspect her of being a witch. Everyone knew that she was good and only had good intentions. An image of Charles Hay flashed in her mind and Meggie felt unsettled. He was the only person she didn't trust. Yet he paid her well for her services. She had no way of refusing Charles Hay's demands. How could she? His father was the most influential man in the village and his son could do no wrong. So long as Charles' reputation remained unsullied, everyone was happy.

Meggie said a quick prayer for the souls she had prevented from being born, and sped up as she hurried to Coventina's Well. 'Blessed Coventina and the Water Nymphs – forgive me. I know what I do is wrong. Yet I have no choice.'

Another image of Charles Hay slipped into her mind; and she quickly blotted it out as she squinted towards the Well, trying to make out the shape she saw by it – she thought it was human, but whether it was male or female, she could not tell. Part of her felt annoyed at the intrusion. Part of her felt intrigued that someone else should be kneeling by the Well, as this figure seemed to be doing. Were they worshipping Coventina as well? She hurried up a little, and stumbled on the uneven ground. She picked herself up again and ran to the Well.

Meggie arrived by the stone structure and looked around the area. Nobody was there. She wondered if it was the same person who had been on the old fort a little while ago. Perhaps they had wandered off into the dip of the valley and disappeared from sight. Ah, well. If they were important, they would come back to her. Instead of worrying about it, she knelt down by the Well and bowed her head in prayer. After a little while, someone spoke to her.

'I thought I would find you here,' The voice was soft and round, full of the rolling nuances of the true Northumbrian. Meggie looked up and smiled.

'Alice!' she said. 'I was just thinking about you.' This was not far from the truth. Alice was the latest girl to suffer at the hands of Charles Hay. She was Meggie's closest friend. It had broken Meggie's heart when she had been approached this time. Alice had asked her first, as soon as she realised. In truth, the brew Meggie had prepared was already working, when Charles had demanded an audience with her. Yet she could not tell Charles this. Alice had sworn her to secrecy and Meggie was loyal to her friends and enemies alike –

everything that needed to be secret, remained a secret. Alice smiled back at her and sat down by her friend, hugging her knees to her chest. Her dark hair was pulled back into a messy braid, accentuating her pretty face and dark blue eyes. Meggie cast an appraising gaze over her friend. She looked older than her seventeen years today. It wasn't surprising, considering what had happened to her recently. Despite her prettiness, her face was pale and there was a sadness about her eyes that hadn't been there last week.

'Are you well, my love?' Meggie asked, sitting back on her heels. 'Mr Hay asked me to check anyway, but I need to know for my own sake. Alice shrugged her shoulders but didn't answer.

She looked out over the countryside and the remains of the fort.'I've always loved it out here,' said Alice, evading the question. 'I'm not surprised you do as well. But it is a strange place.'

Meggie nodded, shredding some flower heads into tiny trumpets, ready to throw into the Well.'It is strange for those folk who do not understand it. For those who do, it is magical.'

Alice laughed, but there was a bitter note to the sound.'Magical. Aye. Things happen out here. Things mortals do not understand. But you are different. You understand the place. You believe in its guardians and its spirits, don't you? Anyway. I came out here to say goodbye to you. I'm leaving, and didn't want to go without telling you.'

'Alice! Where are you going? Are you leaving because of...what's happened?' cried Meggie.

Alice nodded, still staring out at the countryside. 'It can't be helped. I'm sorry to do this to you. I hope you understand,' she said.

'But where will you go?' asked Meggie. 'Is there anything I can do to stop you? Is it him – Charles Hay? Is he making you do this?' Her voice rose hysterically and she felt tears springing to her eyes. She brushed them away angrily. Alice was the only one who truly knew her, who she felt truly comfortable with. What would she do without her? Her Grandmother had died last year, her parents long before that. If Alice left, she would be alone.

'Dear Meggie,' sighed Alice. 'If there was another way, I would seize it.' As if to underline her point, she unfolded her arms from around her knees and leaned towards Meggie. She took Meggie's hands in hers. 'Thank you, Meggie. Know that you did what you could. I'm sorry this had to happen.' Alice raised Meggie's hands to her face. She brought them to her lips and kissed them. Gently, she replaced them on Meggie's knee and smiled at her friend. A tear rolled down Alice's cheek as well. 'I'll see you again, though. Don't be afraid,' she said and stood up. She brushed her dress down and looked at Meggie, who remained kneeling on the grass.

'Alice!' she cried. 'Please...'

Alice shook her head and turned away. She walked off across the valley and over the old fort. Meggie watched her until she disappeared from sight.

'No,' Meggie whispered, suddenly understanding. 'Oh no!' She jumped to her feet and ran as fast as she could back to the village. 'No!' she cried as she left Coventina's Well behind. The flower heads lay scattered across the grass, until a breeze blew up and lifted them off the ground to dance away across the valley.

Meggie arrived back at the village, gasping for breath and red in the face. 'Alice!' she cried as she ran through the dirty track which was the main street of the village. 'Alice!' She pushed her way past a crowd of farmers who were arguing about something and wove her way through the buildings until she came to Alice's house. Before she even reached the door, she heard howls and crying coming from the building and she began to panic.

'My daughter!' cried a woman's voice. 'My only child. My little Alice!' Meggie burst into the small living quarters and ran towards a bed in the corner of the room.

68

Alice lay on the bed white and cold, her black hair fanned out around her pale face. Her eyes were closed and her lips were bloodless. Dark smudges stained the skin beneath her eyes, as if thumbs had been pressed into the hollows and dragged out ugly marks.

'Oh no. Oh no. What happened? What happened to her?' sobbed Meggie, throwing herself onto her knees by the bed. She grasped hold of Alice's hand and tried uselessly to rub some life into it.

Alice's mother cried out and pulled Meggie away from her. 'It's your fault. You did this to her!' she cried. 'You and your potions. I found it. I found the stuff you'd given her. I knew all about it. I could tell. She was different. I guessed what had happened. I knew it was that Hay lad. But we could have done something. Anything would have been better than this! You killed her.'

Meggie stared at her, terrified. Two more women appeared from somewhere in the shadow alcoves by the fireplace and stood glaring at her, arms folded and heads shaking.

'I didn't! She asked me to help her. I did what she wanted...' Meggie looked at all three women. She raised her arms before her and turned her hands palm upwards in the age-old gesture of pleading for one's innocence.

'You killed her!' cried Alice's mother. 'Look at her. Look at her and tell me you weren't responsible...' she howled pitifully and crumpled onto a stool, sobbing pathetically. 'My baby is dead, and it's all your fault,' she said. 'She's dead.'

Meggie ran back to the bed and hung over her friend, searching for some hope, some faint breath or heartbeat that would tell her all this was a mistake. It couldn't be happening. Not to Alice. Not because of what she had done. But it was. Her spirit had come to tell Meggie as much when she had been at the Sacred Well. But she'd also told her she didn't blame her. It had to be the mugwort; Alice had been too weak to take the full strength potion. Why hadn't Meggie thought ahead? Alice was being violently sick, and that was how she had guessed. But Meggie hadn't been sensible, had she? She only wanted to rush in and help her friend. Not only could the mugwort do what Meggie had prepared it for, but it could make you fall asleep. Too much of it- or if the person taking it was too weak - and the drug would numb your senses. It might even lead you into a sleep from which you would never wake. Alice was dead.

'No!' Meggie shouted. 'Alice told me. She doesn't blame me. It's not my fault. She came to me, I was on the moors by the old fort and she...'

'Enough!' screamed Alice's mother. 'Enough of your evil. It is your fault and I blame you.' She pointed at Meggie. 'Get her out of here. Get her and her evil ways out of my house. She killed my daughter. She killed her!' Alice's mother broke into a fresh onslaught of sobbing. One of the women in the house pushed Meggie roughly out into the street. She was, Meggie realised, the widow of a farm labourer, killed in an accident last year. She had a son and two daughters of her own. Three children, all under five years old.

'Don't you dare come back,' the girl hissed. She was barely twenty two. 'Don't you dare turn up at the funeral, you hear me? You've done enough damage as it is.' She looked terrified. And with good reason. Meggie's eyes widened in disbelief. This girl had received the same service from Meggie only three months ago.

'You!' cried Meggie. 'You. How can you do this, Lizzie? How can you believe all this?'

'Just go away,' said Lizzie. 'Just go away.'

Lizzie slammed the wooden door in Meggie's face. Meggie was left standing in the street, scared, lonely and very, very bewildered.

Hidden away in the alley across the street, Charles Hay watched the proceedings with no particular emotion. It wasn't his fault. The girl, Alice, had obviously been weak and sickly anyway. He turned his back on the cottage and mounted his horse. Flicking his crop against its flanks, he trotted away from the village towards the old pack horse route across the moors. It was annoying, but he felt sure he would be protected. Nobody except Meggie and himself knew the truth of the matter. To anybody else, it would just be one of these tragic incidents that happened every now again. He didn't need to worry about it all.

Once clear of the village, he whipped the horse harder and he felt its muscles contract beneath him. He clung on tight as it cantered away, and the fresh Northumbrian air blew all thoughts of Alice from his mind.

# 2010

'Wow!' murmured Liv. She had made her way up the central aisle of the Mithraeum and was leaning over the three altars. She was bending over the altar on the left. A picture of a god was carved onto it and three leaf shapes were punched out of the stone at the side of his head. 'Sunbeams,' said Liv. 'Of course. Mithras is the sun god.' She ran her fingers over the stone. 'The way that was glowing when we came in – like a candle was showing through the beams. Brilliant. Must have been the way the sun was shining through it.'

'I didn't see it,' said Ryan. He had eventually trailed into the ruin after her. He shivered and looked around him. 'Where's the sun gone, anyway? Come on, Mithras!' he bellowed, throwing his head upwards and his arms outwards. 'Let's have some proper sunshine!'

'Hush!' said Liv, turning and glaring at him. 'You shouldn't be shouting on like that here. They wouldn't like it.'

Ryan gave her an odd look.'Who wouldn't like it? The Romans? Like they would still be hanging around here.' He laughed. 'Given the choice between here and Roma, what would you do?'

'You don't know what happened. You don't know anything,' said Liv. 'Because they didn't all come from Roma or even Italia. I told you, they're from all over the empire; Holland and Germany and Spain and Arabia...'

'Wasn't that the line up for the World Cup semi-finals?' Ryan quipped. 'Joke! Joke!' he added quickly as Liv's face grew thunderous. 'Aw,come on, Liv. Lighten up. You've gone all weird. What's up with you?' He walked up to her and tried to take her hand. She shook him off and turned her back on him. She hunched over the altars, studying them. 'Liv?' he asked, but she wouldn't respond. Ryan sighed and sat down where the backpacker lady had been sitting. He stared around him, slouching down and stuffing his hands in his pockets. 'So. Mithras,' he said. 'Tell me more about your people. If you say something, she might respond. It looks like I'm all out of favour.'

'Get out,' a voice said. Quite clearly. And quite close to him.

'Woah!' Ryan swore loudly and jumped to his feet. 'Liv, did you hear that? Did you say something?' Liv turned away from the altars, frowning at him. She had a sheaf of papers in her hand now, and was trying to match the weathered inscriptions on the altars to the information she had gleaned from her research.

'Ryan, pack it in. Stop being so stupid. There's no need to mock me, you know. I tell you what. You go home and I'll finish up here myself. I can't be bothered with you.' She turned back to the altars and hunkered down in front of them. She traced her fingers over the inscription and spelled it out in her head; DEO INVICTO MITRAE M SIMPLICIVS SIMPLEX PREF VSLM

'"To the Invincible God Mithras,"' she whispered, translating it from her papers. '"The prefect Marcus Simplicius Simplex, willingly and deservedly fulfills his vow." Wow. I wonder what his vow was?' She straightened up and looked at the other two altars. For some reason, she wasn't that drawn to those two. They were interesting, of course; but she wanted to linger by this one. Marcus Simplicius Simplex. 'Who were you, Marcus?' Liv wondered out loud. 'And would I have wanted to know you?'

'It was a mistake,' said a voice. Liv spun around, expecting to see Ryan next to her. But he was standing on the raised grass area staring at her in horror.

'There was a bloke next to you,' he said. 'Right next to you. Looking at you. I mean it.'

Liv looked Ryan straight in the eyes.'That's enough!' she shouted. 'Go home, Ryan. Stop making fun of me!'

'I'm not!' cried Ryan. His face was chalky white and his eyes huge and terrified. 'Really. I wish I was making fun of you. But I'm not. I swear it. I'm not making fun of you.'

# 1650

In the days that followed Alice's death, Meggie was terrified at the prospect of leaving her cottage. Whenever she did manage to go out, the whole village seemed to be pointing at her and whispering about her. Conversations would stop as she approached and continue as she hurried away. She had never felt so alone.

Meggie took to spending more time at Coventina's Well than ever. She would pray and cry and ask for forgiveness over and over again. She would even call out for Alice to come back to her; but she never did. She tried once more to speak to Alice's mother, to explain what had happened, but the door was slammed in her face. She snuck into the church for Alice's funeral; a place she had never visited before and never would again. A group of village men spotted her sitting at the back, and manhandled her out of the building. One of them clamped his hand over her mouth to stop her protesting, and another pinned her arms against her side. Meggie was small and slim; it was not necessary for four men to force her out and to contain her struggles. Meggie felt sullied – the men had seemed to enjoy it in some horrible way. She could smell them on her skin for hours; feel their fingers gripping into her flesh and taste the hand that had covered her mouth. Lizzie was sitting three rows from the front; she put her head down and clasped her hands together in prayer as Meggie was thrown out. Meggie noticed her, and thought bitterly that the woman was thanking God it wasn't her body at the front of the church, lying in the simple pine coffin by the altar. The coffin was so small, so tiny. Was Alice really that size? For a moment, Meggie visualized her rounder and softer than she had ever been, with another life curled up inside her. Once outside the church, and in fact outside the stone boundary wall of the church where the men had dragged her to, Meggie had slid to the ground howling uncontrollably. She realised again that it wasn't one life she'd taken, it was two. And Charles Hay was living in blissful denial of this. He knew Alice was dead, of course he did. But Meggie was certain he didn't care one way or another.

Meggie was right. On the day of Alice's funeral, Charles was in Newcastle on business with his father. They had met a gentleman by the name of Cuthbert Nicholson in a local hostelry. This was the man who had become a legend in Newcastle – twenty-seven witches had been identified by him. He was the toast of the city. His methods were questionable, but his work thorough. The witches had been hanged on the town moor and buried in St Andrew's churchyard with metal nails hammered into their knees to prevent them from rising again. It was a necessary evil, Mr Nicholson had told them. Witches were rife. He thought he would be asked to go to Scotland and the borders after this; he had heard that there were some cases he needed to investigate up there. Charles had smiled into his ale. Dear Meggie; he hoped she would steer well clear of Mr Nicholson. He might need her services again in the future. Although, having said that, the more he thought about Meggie, the more he wondered what she would be like as a lover. She wasn't the most beautiful girl in the village, but he thought she had potential. She would be feeling rather vulnerable after her friend's sad demise as well. Perhaps she would welcome a little chat with him. A little fun. It would take her mind off things, that was certain.

Yes, Charles Hay was in a rather positive mood as he took to his bed in the inn that night. He had paid his lady-friend well for her services and she had melted away into the darkness of the streets. But the whole time, he had imagined Meggie's body beneath his; Meggie's eyes meeting his as they moved together. He had suppressed a smile. She had that funny little squint when she looked at you; she put her head on one side and creased her eyes up at the corners. It was rather attractive, in an odd sort of way. But perhaps at such close quarters, she wouldn't need to squint. A good wash and some clean clothes, the girl would be as good as a Lady and quite presentable. He lay down on the feather mattress with his hands behind his head, staring at the drapes above him. Yes; Meggie would be very interesting. He would have to work on fulfilling that ambition when he got back home. Charles closed his eyes and slept with a smile on his face; confidence is a wonderful thing and the best narcotic in the world.

# AD 391

'All hail!' It was two months into the New Year. Saturnalia was all but a memory, and today Marcus had commanded the auxiliaries in his troops to stand to attention and welcome the Praefectus castrorum; the new Commandant. As a prefect himself, Marcus was in charge of a group of men but had no imperium- no immense power, such as this man had. Marcus stood at the head of his troops staring straight ahead of him. Janus was opposite him, in front of his group of men. And so it continued throughout the centre of the fort. The gates of Carrawburgh swung open and the horse which carried the new Commandant to his posting at the edge of the empire paraded through the entrance. A stocky, middle aged man sat in the saddle. His hair was shorn close to his head and peppered with silver. His eyes scanned the troops, seemingly noticing anything and anyone that might be out of place. Titus Perpetuus had been warned that this might be a challenging position, yet he was ready and willing to meet it. He had not risen through the ranks by shying away from difficulty. He followed Emperor Theodosius diligently; it was the only way. Christianity had started to bleed into the empire a while ago, strange beliefs creeping in and being met with suspicion from the Pagan Romans. Thanks to Emperor Constantine and his Edict of Milan, Christianity had been tolerated in the empire since 313. Theodosius was gradually stamping out the Pagan beliefs, and this was one of the reasons Titus had been sent here. Information had come through that worried him – the cult of Mithras was growing in these Northern territories, they still worshipped at the bog-spring which had been dedicated to Coventina the water nymph; they still had a shrine to some more water nymphs by this heathen temple. It was all wrong. Things would have to change.

In the cart behind the Commandant a small, sharp-featured woman looked out over the men; the Commandant's wife. Her eyes darted back and forth across the troops, noticing a lot of the men were lighter skinned and fairer haired than she was used to. The Batavians. Of course; they were a Germanic people. One or two were dark haired like herself and her daughter.

Aemelia sat by her mother, warmly encased in animal skins and looking around her curiously. Carrawburgh was the same as any other fort, really. Aemelia knew her family would have a villa on the site, she knew mostly what the days would consist of. It was always interesting coming to a new posting with her family, though. She had spent her whole life travelling from one fort to another with them. Things had changed a little over those eighteen years; but not too much. But she had never been to anywhere as remote as this place. The fields stretched out endlessly beyond Carrawburgh. Somewhere to the North were the wild Pictish people. Aemelia had heard tales about these tribes. They covered themselves in blue woad, believing it would defend them from the Roman attacks; and what they lacked in battle strategy, or even weapons, they made up for in bravery. Or stupidity, depending on how you viewed it. She put her head down and smiled to herself, imagining the Picts running up to this fort, ready to attack the wall. She imagined them stopping dead at the vallum, wondering what they could do next to negotiate the great ditch which was hollowed out before the wall. She guessed they would shout a lot and jump around a lot. They would stand no chance against these soldiers.

Aemelia raised her deep brown eyes and stared around at the men as the cart rumbled past them. Her gaze alighted on one of the Prefects, a tall, fair man, standing to attention. For a moment, his expression wavered as he caught her eye.

Marcus was a trained soldier, a professional man. But even he couldn't control the little flip his stomach made when the girl drove past him.

Titus Perpetuus missed nothing. His eyes narrowed slightly and he mentally noted the tall, fair Prefect.

Janus allowed himself a small smile as the cart passed his men. He missed nothing, either.

# 1650

'Cuthbert Nicholson. Are you willing to assist us further afield?' The row of magistrates sat on a long wooden bench, staring at the man in front of them. Cuthbert Nicholson was a tall, imposing man. He favoured black clothing and stood like an immense bird of prey before the city dignitaries.

He tapped his wooden staff on the floor thoughtfully, then raised it up and weighed it between his hands. 'How much?' he asked. His voice was deep and throaty. The measured tones had driven fear into the heart of Newcastle's under-classes. Twenty-seven citizens had met their fate, albeit indirectly, by his word.

'Twenty shillings per witch,' replied the chief dignitary.

'And where would I be travelling to?' asked Nicholson.

'Scotland.'

Nicholson laughed and shook his head. 'No. I shall not travel through those border lands unprotected. You must find yourself another man. I refuse to do that for such a paltry sum of money.' He turned and made to leave the room.

'Wait! Mr Nicholson. Perhaps we can come to some arrangement? There is a like-minded gentleman we would be interested to meet, a Mr John Kincaid. We have had word from our fellows in Dalkeith that he has done a great deal of good these last few years. We want you to bring him to us. He shares your concerns and Christian values.' The magistrate leaned forward and interwove his fingers. 'What would persuade you to travel north for our purposes?'

Nicholson paused, tapping his fingers with the filthy, bitten nails off the door frame. 'Safe passage to Scotland and back would be a pre-requisite, of course,' he said thoughtfully. Then he turned and fixed the magistrate with his heavy, hooded eyes. 'And a payment of three pounds, per head, of each and every witch I convict. I shall travel north through all your market towns and small villages. I shall flush them out for you on my way. But it must be worth my while. It is what God wills. These wenches are well-documented in country villages.'

The magistrate nodded, and conferred with his colleagues. They men bent their heads close together, their grey, curled wigs nodding like sheep in unison at muttered comments. Finally, they broke apart. Nicholson remained by the door, waiting politely for the response.

'We agree to your terms, Mr Nicholson. This evil is widespread. If you are willing to bring trials to these villages, three pounds per head is a reasonable sum to pay.'

'You will not be disappointed,' said Nicholson. He nodded at the magistrates and took his leave. 'Good day, gentlemen. I trust you will arrange my escorts forthwith?'

'Leave it with us, Sir. Good day. And may God go with you.'

Nicholson made the sign of the cross and bowed to the magistrates. Then he turned and left the room, closing the door softly behind him.

# AD 391

'It is true, faithful ones. The new Commandant is a Christian,' said the Pater. The men were reclining on the benches in the Mithraeum. The detritus of their feast surrounded them and it was Marcus' job as the Corax to clear up. He moved between the men, emptying flagons of wine into goblets so he could tidy up.

'It is more important than ever that we protect our identities. Let nobody know you are a member of the cult. Tell nobody your rank,' continued the Pater. Marcus felt himself flushing. He needed to make a conscious effort to rein himself in. Janus was still waiting for his invitation to join and had been pressing Marcus for information.

'Perhaps, with Titus Perpetuus here, the cult will need more men?' Janus had asked eagerly. 'Will that be a factor in my initiation? I am willing to enter the cult as soon as they need me. We can be strong and fight against this Christian. He is here to change things, and I do not like to think about what he might try and do.' He had looked across at the temple as he took up his watch, then further afield towards the Sacred Well. 'Remind me to make an offering to Coventina,' he said. 'The more deities we have on our side, the better.'

'I am inclined to agree,' said Marcus,' but here is not the place to discuss it. We must do our duty to the fort and consider the implications later.' Janus had shot a glance at him in surprise. It was unlike Marcus to deflect a conversation, whether it was at a change of watch or not.

'Marcus! Where does your allegiance lie?' hissed Janus. 'To Carrawburgh fort with this Christian in charge, or to your religion? You can be moved to a different fort as easily as day follows night. But your religion and your beliefs go with you. Unless, of course, you choose to follow Christianity and become Titus' lapdog?'

'I do not like your attitude,' snapped Marcus. 'It is not the place to discuss this.' Janus opened his eyes wide.

'But what is the problem?' he asked, confused and hurt by Marcus' outburst. Marcus was one of the most good-natured, trusting people Janus had ever met. Sometimes, he felt this personality did not sit well with a Prefect of Marcus' rank. Janus was more forthright and confident than Marcus; sometimes Janus had a definite swagger to his walk, a way of fixing a person with a stare that was both quizzical and challenging, yet somehow inviting respect and honesty from the recipient. Marcus was much more relaxed. He radiated common sense and openness, drawing people in like a moth to a flame. They were both excellent leaders; yet where Janus seemed to have been born into leadership and the role appeared to have evolved to accommodate him, Marcus had worked his way up the ranks. Janus could not remember the last time Marcus had been short with him. What had changed?

Janus had looked around him, shaking his head almost imperceptibly, as if he could find the answer to his friend's behaviour in the wild moors and hills around him. Then he saw it; maybe not in the moors, but a little closer to home. Aemelia, the Commandant's daughter, was walking across the square in the centre of the fort. She was heading towards the gate, escorted by a slave who was carrying her basket. She must be going into the vicus. This girl was allowed more freedom than Janus thought was usual. She often wandered around the fort or disappeared into the civilian settlement. Janus had even spotted her walking across the moors alone. He doubted that Titus Perpetuus knew his only child was walking about the northern territory in such a fashion. His sharp eyes spotted Marcus cast a glance her way and pull himself up straighter as she hurried past them. He also saw Aemelia look up under her eyelashes at the men standing on the ramparts, a smile playing around her rosy lips. Her gaze was only for Marcus,

Janus realised. This, then, was what had changed. He would not let Marcus know he had realised yet. But at least he had an explanation for his friend's behaviour. Not that it was a secret he was happy about knowing. Janus frowned as he walked down the steps and left Marcus patrolling the wall. Things were definitely changing at Carrawburgh. He wondered how this would affect the cult of Mithras and Marcus' role in that.

Marcus was wondering much the same thing as he moved around the temple after the feast. The worship of Mithras was not at the forefront of his mind any more: and he knew it was something he was loathe to admit to anybody.

# AD 391

Aemelia was alone today; at last she had escaped from her mother and the slave she insisted accompanied her daughter everywhere. She checked over her shoulder as she slipped out of the fort gate, then sighed. She had thought she was alone. Syrus, her slave, had other ideas. He was there again, tailing her. He followed at a discreet distance, stopping in the shadows every so often and waiting for her to move on. There was no escape from him. It was like having a bodyguard, she thought. And for what reason? She only wanted to visit the vicus again. It was not as if she was going to come to any harm in the little village.

Aemelia enjoyed wandering around the market stalls and peeping into the taverns. She loved the smells of the meals cooking in the houses, the sound of the children laughing and playing in the little forum whilst their mothers chatted. Occasionally she would see a soldier from Carrawburgh, slipping into certain buildings furtively, or leaving them with a kiss and a wave from a woman who was wrapped only in a blanket. Aemelia couldn't help smiling. Everyone knew exactly what was going on; yet some of these men tried so hard to hide it. Why, most of these children belonged to serving auxiliary soldiers in the cohort. The families were happy to wait until their men had completed their service, before they could be married and granted Roman citizenship. The Officers were more fortunate. They had quarters in the fort with their families and slaves. Marriage was legal for them. Aemelia always loved it when babies were born within the walls of the forts– it was always a cause for great celebration. And although her father was a devout Christian, he turned a blind eye to the offerings and prayers the families made to the Pagan deities who had blessed them in such a way.

Aemelia had grown up surrounded by men on the forts. She had changed from a chubby, dark-haired toddler, always ready with a smile for the soldiers, through the awkwardness of youth where she blushed and stammered should anyone address her and finally to the beautiful, confident young woman she was now. She enjoyed exploring new places and meeting new people. Any change in her father's post was a God-given opportunity. She particularly loved it up here. It still amused her to think of the Picts trying to storm the Wall; but to be fair she had never seen any of them attempt it.

Aemelia wound her way down the path to the vicus and headed towards the village; for, to all intents and purposes, a village was what it had become. She walked towards a large, stone wall, which formed the edge of a square building. She leaned over the side and rested her hands on the wall as she sniffed deeply. This place had a special smell – sort of fresh and pure. She couldn't explain it any better. Water bubbled within it, and like the shrine to the water nymphs by that awful temple, it was open to the elements. It was obviously a shrine as well, or something sacred at least; it had that feeling about it. Aemelia shivered slightly – it always had that effect on her. She didn't know if part of it was guilt. Lenient though her father was with his soldiers, he was less lenient with her. He made her wear a gold cross around her neck and had taught her to be proud of her Christianity. It was nothing to be ashamed of, he told her. Aemelia knew that; yet she couldn't help but be fascinated by this shrine. A man walked past her and threw a coin into the water, muttering something as he did so. Aemelia watched the coin sink into the pool and wondered what he had thanked the goddess for. She saw a stone carving leaning up against the wall, depicting a woman reclining on what might have been the edge of stream. There were several smaller altars lining the walls. They showed carvings of leaves and wreathes and patterns and even people. She wondered again what the significance was. There was a carving showing three people at the other shrine. It was enormous; but this one wasn't quite so big.

'Do you find this interesting?' said a voice close by her ear. She jumped and turned to see another man smiling shyly at her. It was the fair haired man she had noticed on her first day here.

'Oh! I'm sorry – am I in the way? Do you need to be in here?' asked Aemelia stepping back. 'Please – don't let me stop you.' She waved her arm towards the entrance and smiled.

'No, I do not need to be in there. I have no need of the goddess today,' smiled the young man. 'Forgive me; aren't you the Commandant's daughter?'

Aemelia laughed. 'It is very obvious, Sir, that I am,' she said, bowing slightly. 'My name is Aemelia. I am very different to these lovely ladies of the vicus. I do not feel that I blend in particularly well here.'

'Only because they are used to this weather,' said the man. He indicated her wraps. She had several layers of furs around her body and looked like she could have used some more, had she been given the opportunity.

'Hmm, yes. My attire sets me apart somewhat,' said Aemelia. 'That and the fact that my teeth are chattering and my nose is red.'

'It gets colder,' warned her companion. 'Much colder. This place,' he indicated the Well, 'is dedicated to our marvellous goddess Coventina. She helps, amongst other things, to melt the ice and snow and bring back running water to the countryside. She is a water nymph, but a very special one. Her name means "the memory of snow".'

'How lovely!' cried Aemelia. She tugged the animal skins closer to her and fixed the man with a look. 'So I know that this is Coventina, and you know that I am Aemelia. I do not know who you are, though. Would you be so kind as to enlighten me?'

'Certainly.' The man bowed. 'My name is Marcus Simplicius Simplex. I am a Prefect in the Batavian Cohort, stationed at Carrawburgh. But you will know where I hail from, no doubt.'

'I had my suspicions, Prefect,' smiled Aemelia. 'Are you free for a little while, perhaps? I would like to become better acquainted with the vicus. You have already explained Coventina's Well to me. I should like you to escort me around the area and point out some places of interest.'

'That would be my pleasure,' said Marcus. 'But will your father be agreeable to it? I should hate to think that I was crossing boundaries...'

'No boundaries,' said Aemelia. 'I am new to the area. I am being escorted and advised by a soldier in my father's cohort. You are looking after me, a stranger, in a new place. He cannot complain about that, can he? And besides,' she nodded pointedly behind her where an olive skinned man stood half-hidden amongst some tall ferns. 'My dear slave Syrus never lets me wander far from his sight.'

'Then we have no issues. It is perfectly reasonable that I should escort you, under the eagle eye of Syrus,' said Marcus. He raised his hand in acknowledgment to Syrus and offered Aemelia his other arm. 'Come with me, young lady, and I shall protect you.'

Marcus had originally intended to go to the Mithraic temple to give thanks to the sun god. It was a brighter day, today, despite it being cold and blustery; the icy wind that blew from the north had not brought snow as they had feared. But he contented himself with throwing a coin into Coventina's Well, and sent a silent prayer to her instead, thanking her for the absence of snow and ice.

Marcus and Aemelia did not see a man standing at the door of Aelia's house, watching them walk away from the Well and in the opposite direction to the temple. The Pater watched them disappear behind a building and narrowed his eyes. He had expected Marcus to come to the temple today. He had mentioned that he would be there. It was almost time for the Corax's next initiation ceremony and the Pater needed to let him know.

# AD 391

'She is rather attractive, is she not?' asked Janus. Marcus dipped his head and coloured. The disagreement on the ramparts long forgotten, Janus and Marcus had slipped easily back into their friendship.

'I do not know who you are referring to, my friend,' Marcus replied, busying himself with mending the leather thongs on his sandals. He had spent the morning on drill and practising swordsmanship. It was not his turn for watch yet, so he had taken the opportunity to tend to his kit.

'Our Commandant's beautiful daughter, of course,' said Janus. 'I believe she is called Antonia?'

'Aemelia,' responded Marcus, too quickly.

'Ha! So she has been worthy of your notice, then?' laughed Janus, nudging him good-naturedly.

'Perhaps,' smiled Marcus. Janus knew him too well. He couldn't bluff with him for very long.

'Then tell me, what do you propose to do about it?' asked Janus, more seriously now. 'It would never be allowed; you understand that, don't you?' Marcus pulled the needle through the sandals and didn't answer. He shrugged. He knew that Aemelia was only eighteen.

Janus shook his head and looked at Marcus with concern in his eyes. 'Be sensible, Marcus,' he said. Marcus ignored him and tugged the leather thongs to test them. He turned and reached for a small, bone-handled knife and cut the thread off.

'You are a stubborn man,' sighed Janus. 'When will you learn to take advice?'

'I will never take advice from you,' smiled Marcus. 'You should know that by now.' Janus rolled his eyes.

'Yes. You are a difficult man indeed. So if you will not listen to me, you must tell me more. What is it about Antonia...'

'...Aemelia...'

'...Aemelia, that you like?'

'Ah, Janus,' implored Marcus. 'Do not make me do this! It is wrong that I should even have confided in you! Forget I said anything. Look. There is Felix, coming to seek you out.'

Janus looked up and saw one of his men walking towards him.

Felix stood tall and straight before the men and waited to be acknowledged.

Janus nodded at him. 'What is it?' he asked the soldier.

'The Commandant has issued a request that we convene in two hours at the principia,' he said. The principia was the headquarters of the fort. The Cohort met every morning there, and it was unusual that the Commandant should want another meeting. Marcus and Janus looked at one another.

'And did he advise you why this was the case?' asked Janus, sitting back and looking at Felix curiously.

'No, Sir. But I believe a messenger arrived this morning.'

'Whilst we were training, perhaps. Very well. Thank you. You are dismissed.'

Felix nodded and marched away from the officers.

'Interesting,' said Janus. 'I did not see anyone come. Did you?'

Marcus shook his head. 'No. Well, it should be interesting what he needs to report,' he said. Plus, he knew if they were at the headquarters, it was only a stone's throw to where Aemelia was in the praetor, the Commandant's house. Perhaps he would be lucky enough to see her. He smiled to himself. He felt in the pouch that he carried around his waist. Perhaps he would have time to give her his gift before the meeting.

Janus stood up and stretched. 'Will you be visiting the temple soon?' he asked Marcus. 'I was wondering if...'

'In the name of the gods, Janus!' said Marcus. 'I have told you; the Pater will let you know when he can initiate you.'

THE MEMORY OF SNOW

'I know,' sighed Janus, holding his hands up. 'You are right, my friend. But I have a feeling that this little talk by the Commandant will not help our cause. I am anxious to do my part for Mithras. He has been good to us. Please. If I go to the temple now, will you come with me? I would like to see if I can contact the Pater myself; or at least see if there is some way I can leave a message for him. Is it true that there is a secret place to leave messages for members of the cult?'

Marcus sighed. He looked up at his friend. Janus was rocking back and forth on the balls of his feet now, his hands behind his back; a sure sign that he was anxious to get moving.

He smiled engagingly at Marcus.'Please?' asked Janus.

'All right. I will come with you. But I have to return in good time. I have things I need to do.'

'I understand,' said Janus. 'Time, tide and Antonia wait for no man.'

Marcus didn't bother to correct him. 'Come. If you want to go, we have to go now,' he said.

'So, there is a secret place for contact?' asked Janus. 'Wait! I need something to write on.' He looked around and patted his tunic as if a wax tablet and stylus would leap out at him from nowhere.

'There are implements at the temple,' sighed Marcus. He stood up and cast a glance at the

Commandant's house. Was she in? He would make certain he caught her later. But he might as well humour Janus for now. Perhaps if Janus left a message, the Pater would contact him directly and he would stop asking Marcus about his initiation.

The two men left the fort and headed down to the temple. The path was slippery with the rain that had fallen earlier that day and Marcus knew the temple would feel damp and cold once they were inside it. It never seemed welcoming when there were no people in it. Aemelia hated the place. He had taken her down to it once, to show her what he believed in. She loved Coventina's Well and adored the Shrine to the Water Nymphs, so he thought she would like the temple. He was wrong. She had refused to enter it, shaking her head as Marcus paused at the door, ready to open it for her.

'No, I do not want to come in. It is a horrible place,' she had said, pulling her arm away from his and walking deliberately away from the temple and towards the Water Nymph shrine. 'I shall wait here. Anyway, I am sure women are not allowed in your temple.'

'Well, no. They are not usually allowed in,' said Marcus frowning. 'But I think the men would make an exception for you, just so you can see what it is like inside. You are the Commandant's daughter, after all.'

'Yes, and we are a Christian family,' said Aemelia. 'Don't think I haven't heard the whispered comments or the complaints about us. I am invisible to a lot of these men. They think because I am a young woman I do not understand them. But I do. They would rather we had not come to your Carrawburgh.'

'I don't feel like that!' cried Marcus walking up to her. He took her hands in his and looked into her eyes. 'Truly. I am happy that you are here. Perhaps more happy than you know.'

Aemelia had ducked her head, but not before he had seen her smile.

'I know you are happy, Prefect,' she said. 'As I am happy to be here. But it does not make this awful building any more bearable. Even if it is important to you.'

'It is important to me. Of course it is,' said Marcus looking over his shoulder at the building. Then he turned back to face Aemelia. He looked down at her, his eyes softening. 'But not as important as you are. If you feel uncomfortable here, I shall not go in. We can go back to the vicus and find something to eat or drink. I don't want you to feel like that.'

Aemelia smiled at him and squeezed his hands. 'Thank you, but you don't have to avoid it because of me. It is such a dark, eerie place. It just feels wrong to me,' she said.

'Sssh. No. We will leave. Don't worry about it,' said Marcus. 'Come on.' He dropped her hands and offered her his arm. She took it and smiled up at him.

'Thank you,' she said. He smiled down at her and they began to walk away from the temple, up towards the vicus.

When they had disappeared over the hill, the heavy wooden door of the temple cracked open. The Leo who had been making an offering to Mithras had heard Marcus. He watched to make sure they weren't coming back, then closed the door and sat down inside the temple. The Corax perhaps needed his next initiation now more than ever. He might mention it to the Pater, he thought. Just so the Corax was gently brought back into the fold. It wouldn't do any harm.

Marcus pushed open the door of the temple and looked into the gloom. 'Hello?' he called. 'Are there any servants of Mithras here? Any men who are willing to do their duty to the sun god?' Nothing answered him except a black silence. He waited a moment until his eyes adjusted to the darkness, then beckoned Janus inside. 'Come. We will leave a message and hope that the Pater finds it in his heart to answer you.'

Janus nodded, silhouetted in the grey light outside the door. 'Thank you for coming with me,' he whispered, squeezing in beside Marcus who still held the door open. Marcus pushed a block of stone against the door to prop it open so some light filtered through. 'In the name of the gods...' muttered Janus looking around him. 'It is nothing like I expected.'

'What did you expect?' laughed Marcus. 'It is a temple. That is all.'

'But it is like a cave; it is a sacred cave!' said Janus, his voice echoing around the building.

'Yes. Mithras was born from a rock within a cave,' said Marcus. 'That is why we worship in places like these. Come. Let us leave the message and go. It is never very pleasant when there is nobody else around. It is very different when we have a ceremony. You will see. Now – here is the chest which contains the writing equipment. Write your message and I shall place it where the Pater will find it.'

Janus took the stylus and the wax tablet from Marcus. The tablet consisted of two frames of wood laced together, filled with wax. Any messages could be written then erased, and this preserved the secrecy of the contents. Janus thought for a moment, tapping the stylus on the stone altar.

'No. Janus. Not the altar. Please, don't tap on the altar,' said Marcus, stifling a laugh.

'Oh! Oh dear. I am sorry,' said Janus, looking horrified. 'Forgive me Mithras!' He moved away from the altar and bent over a stone bench. He scraped his message into the wax tablet and folded it up with a small thud. He handed it to Marcus, along with the stylus. Marcus replaced the stylus in the chest and felt around in the wall. All the cult members had access to this secret area. They were bound to read the messages as part of their duty, and also to act upon them as necessary.

'Ah!' said Janus. 'I knew it! Yet it is hardly the cursus publicus is it?' He was referring to the very efficient postal system. Messages and dispatches were sent through various messengers and various postal houses along the route to their destination. In extreme cases, one messenger had to travel throughout the whole empire, stopping at these places on the way for a change of horse and a bed for the night. Less important mail came via oxen and changed hands frequently along the route. Marcus snorted with suppressed laughter and dislodged a large, rectangular brick. He reached into the gap and his fingers touched something hard and cold. Someone had already left a tablet there.

Marcus pulled it out and put Janus' tablet in its place.'Excuse me for one moment,' Marcus said. 'Cursus publicus it may not be, but it serves our purpose. Let me read this.'

Marcus took the tablet to the doorway and opened it up in the light, leaving Janus staring around the temple in awe, fingering things here and there.

'Leave the artefacts alone,' called Marcus, his eyes never leaving the tablet. He heard Janus apologise again, but he was more interested in the wax tablet. What he saw made his heart beat faster.

*Corax Marcus Simplicius Simplex. The Pater decrees that you shall be initiated to the rank of Nymphus, the bridegroom. Your protecting deity from that day forth shall be Venus. This ceremony is to take place on the market day in March. This is the second time the Pater has decreed your initiation. It has been observed that you did not attend the original ceremony, although the information was displayed for you in good time. Remember – you are a servant of Mithras and as such should do his bidding. There will be no third chance.*

Marcus wasted no time in returning to the chest and seizing the stylus. He wrote his acknowledgement of the message on the bottom of the tablet, frowning as he pushed the tablet back into the hole and replaced the brick. It was market day today. He dreaded to think what might have happened had he not visited the temple with Janus.

'You scare me, my friend,' said Janus, opening his eyes wide. 'Did that tablet contain bad news?'

'It was good news,' said Marcus. 'And it may also prove good news for you. Soon, the cult of

Mithras will need a new Corax. Your request could not have been timed better.'

'Are you certain of this?' asked Janus, clutching the top of Marcus' arms. 'Truthfully? You think I may be called upon?'

'You may be,' said Marcus. 'I have much to thank you for, my friend. Had I not come here today with you, things may have been very different. I have missed an important ceremony. Yet I must apologise to you as well. You could have been initiated much sooner had I not been so lax in my duties.' Marcus was mentally thanking the gods for guiding him to the temple today. But he was puzzled and confused. How had he missed the ceremony? When had he neglected his duties and not entered the temple? Then he remembered; it was the day he had brought Aemelia down and she had refused to enter the building. That had been another auspicious day in the Roman calendar. He was willing to bet his last few denarii that his original ceremony had been planned for then. It had been instilled in him that he must not neglect his duties, he must follow orders and act upon things promptly. Mithras would not wait for him.

'You must not tell anyone of this development,' Marcus said to Janus. 'It is secret. You understand that, don't you?'

Janus nodded.'I shall not breathe a word,' he said.

Marcus clapped him on the back and walked towards the wooden door. He bent down and moved the stone away from the door, ushering Janus out in front of him. Janus walked back to the fort with an extra swagger in his step and Marcus followed him, checking his leather pouch again. He still had time before the meeting with the Commandant. He still had time to see Aemelia and give her the gift. And he must return to the temple later for his initiation.

The two men headed back to the fort, both thinking their own thoughts about the Mithraic Cult. Marcus saw a figure bundled up in furs flitting around the market stalls, fingering the jewellery on display and chatting to the traders. Keeping a respectable distance, was her slave.    'Excuse me, my friend,' said Marcus. 'There is something I need to attend to in the vicus.' He broke away from Janus and took the pathway into the village. Janus watched him walk off and approach the girl at the jewellery stall. He stood for a minute or so, seeing the body language between the couple and the dismissal of the slave. Marcus and Aemelia – for that was who Janus knew it was – disappeared into the crowd, and eventually Janus turned back towards the fort.

# AD 391

'Aemelia, would you mind if we went somewhere a little less crowded?' asked Marcus. 'Marcus! I did not expect to see you here today,' said Aemelia. 'But I must say, it is a very pleasant surprise. Olivia, you are dismissed for the moment. Give me some time with this Prefect; we have business to discuss.' A red-headed slave-girl bowed and stepped aside, holding the basket of goods Aemelia had bought. Marcus nodded at the slave-girl, and guided Aemelia away from the jewellery stall with a light touch on her arm.

'You have a different companion today,' he said. 'Where is Syrus?'

'Father has use of him elsewhere. I now have Olivia to protect me.' She rolled her eyes. 'The girl is simple. She does what I tell her to do.' Marcus laughed.

'I prefer you to be guarded by Syrus,' he said. 'He is a good man. I can tell. He would never leave you on your own with a soldier.'

'Syrus was my shadow,' smiled Aemelia. 'It was very inconvenient. Sometimes, I like to be free.'

'It is good to be free. But you also need to be safe,' replied Marcus.

'I have no fear of anybody here!' cried Aemelia. 'I do not need a babysitter. Syrus used to lurk around in the shadows, watching me. He never let me go far on my own. You know that as well as I do. I would often see little leaves waving around in the bushes, or hear twigs snapping. It was all so annoying!'

'Syrus is a good man,' laughed Marcus. 'He would never risk any harm coming to you. You are too precious. But then, I am pleased Olivia has left us. You need not fear me.' He took Aemelia through an alleyway between two houses and they came out behind the buildings. Aemelia could hear water trickling gently behind some trees and followed Marcus as he pushed his way through a gap in the greenery.

She gasped in wonder and looked around her 'Where is this place?' she asked. 'I did not know this existed!' They were standing in a small garden area. A fountain stood in the middle of a pebbled square, and statues were dotted around the four edges. It was too early in the year for flowers, but Aemelia knew that come the summer months, the place would be a profusion of blooms.

'Do you like it?' asked Marcus. 'It belongs to Aelia and her sisters. Look; this is the back of their home.' He pointed to one of the walls which formed the square. 'They keep it as a kind of secret place; a trysting garden, if you like. Only a few people know about it.' He smiled. 'I shall confess that this is not the first time I have visited this place, but it is the first time I have brought anyone special here.'

'Am I special?' asked Aemelia. Feeling bold, she moved closer. She took his hands in hers. Without taking her eyes off him, she raised his hands to her lips and kissed them. 'I hope I am special to you,' she said.

'More special than you can imagine, dear Aemelia,' he answered. He couldn't even think about blaming her for missing his initiation ceremony; he knew he would have done the same again. No, he could only blame himself for that one. He should have returned to the temple without her later on. It had been his own fault.

Their hands still together, Marcus drew Aemelia towards him and returned the kiss; but this time he kissed her on the lips. When they finally drew apart, Aemelia opened her eyes and smiled up at Marcus.

'Well, now. That was rather unexpected,' she said. 'I think I like this trysting garden.' She looked around her again; the colours seemed less grey, the tinkling of the water more magical then before. 'I always thought Coventina's Well would be our special place,' she said thoughtfully. 'It is where we first met, after all.'

'No, I believe Carrawburgh was our first meeting place,' smiled Marcus. Aemelia wrinkled her nose.

'Perhaps. But somewhere like the Well has a far better memory for me. That is where you first spoke to me. And here; this is where you first kissed me.' She tilted her head to one side. 'I don't suppose you would like to do it again?' she asked.

'I could easily be convinced,' murmured Marcus and bent down to her once more. Aemelia gave herself up to him willingly, knowing that nobody would disturb them in the garden. She had been attracted to soldiers before, it was only natural; but Marcus was the first one she had ever felt like this about. It was like she had come home, like the missing part of her suddenly slotted into place. But with the realisation came a kind of sorrow. Marcus was a Pagan, and one of her father's troops as well. She could see no easy way to build on this relationship. What sort of future would they have together? She shook her head to clear her thoughts, trying to dampen them down so she didn't spoil the moment for herself.

'Dear Marcus,' she whispered and laid her head on his shoulder, resting it in the crook of his neck. 'What will become of us, do you think?' Marcus lifted his hand and stroked her dark hair. It was thick and springy beneath his fingers, and he stared out over the garden as he considered her question.

'Truthfully, I do not know,' he said eventually. 'But I want you to have something, so whatever happens in the future, you can look at it and remember me and Carrawburgh and this garden. Would you accept a gift from me?'

Aemelia pulled away from him. 'Of course!' she said. 'I would be honoured to accept a gift from you.'

Marcus smiled and opened the leather pouch he had tied around his waist. 'I had it made especially,' he said, smiling at Aemelia. 'I hope you like it.'

Marcus put his hand into the pouch and brought out a tiny, golden ring. Aemelia gasped, the delicately carved item incongruous in his strong, weather-worn hand. A design had been punched in the ring to form a string of letters. Aemelia hesitated for a moment, then picked the ring out of Marcus' palm. She turned it over and spelled out the letters. AEMELIA ZESES.

'Aemelia may you live,' whispered Aemelia. 'It is beautiful! And so precious. Thank you!' She kissed Marcus again. 'But tell me; why zeses? That is Greek! You are from the Germanic regions, are you not?'

Marcus nodded. 'I am from the Germanic regions,' he said. 'But my craftsman friend tried to translate our Latin word vivas into Greek, then back again.' He shrugged and suddenly laughed at the thought. 'I do not know why! But, whatever he did it for, that is the reason for zeses. I thought you would like it; doesn't vivas in deo mean may you live in God? I am hoping that your God will protect you and help you in all you endeavour to do, as my gods and goddesses protect me. Go on. Put it on. Just on that delicate, smallest finger of yours. It is a token of my love for you. I hope you receive it in the spirit in which it was given.' He bowed at her solemnly and she giggled. She held up her right hand and flexed the little finger.

'Perfect,' she said. 'You have an eye for jewellery, Sir. Or did someone else advise you on what to buy? Your friend Janus, for instance. He seems to be a popular choice of companion for the ladies in the vicus.'

'Ah yes, my good friend Janus. No, it was not his idea. But you are right. The ladies in the vicus look forward to Janus having free time. If we could stop him gambling, he could spend even more time with them.'

'Perhaps he gambles to control the hordes?' suggested Aemelaia with a smile. 'If he is gambling, he cannot amuse the ladies.'

'Very true,' agreed Marcus. 'But enough of Janus. I want to speak of Aemelia.'

'What do you want to speak to her of?' teased Aemelia.

'I just want to know whether she feels the same about me as I do about her. If I know that, at least I can carry some hope with me into the future.'

'She does feel the same,' whispered Aemelia. 'But neither of us knows what the future will hold.'

'Do you believe that we can change the future?' asked Marcus, taking her face in his and running his thumbs down the side of it tenderly. Aemelia closed her eyes and caught a tiny breath.

'I don't know,' she repeated. 'But please, let us not spoil the present with such talk...' Her words died on her lips as Marcus kissed her again, more deeply and slowly than before. He drew away eventually.

'In a few years I will have left the army. Maybe then, if it is meant to be, our gods will guide us. I can wait,' he said.

'As can I,' whispered Aemelia, and gave herself up to the moment, driving all thoughts of the future away.

# AD 391

The men were arranged in the headquarters ready and waiting for the Commandant's address. Marcus had managed to return on time, although he was aware of Janus looking at him quizzically as the troops lined up in the principia. In fact, Marcus realised, he wasn't just looking at him quizzically; there was something else there as well. A sort of disgust and repulsion was evident in Janus' eyes. Janus didn't agree with their relationship, that much was clear. Well, Marcus thought, Janus would just have to accept it. Neither he nor Aemelia had any intention of changing anything. Marcus pressed his lips together firmly and stood so he was not looking directly at his friend. He would deal with the fall-out later. The Commandant was heading to the plinth in the centre of the square anyway. He looked stern and Marcus had a bad feeling about the news that was to come. Perhaps the First Batavian Cohort were to be posted elsewhere? Perhaps he was about to be separated from Aemelia? His heart began to pound as several different scenarios played through his head.

'Men of the First Batavian Cohort,' said the Commandant. His voice was strong and authoritative. 'I have gathered you together to hear news from our Emperor, Theodosius.' His eyes scanned the troops. For a moment, Marcus felt as if the Commandant's eyes settled on him, but then, just as swiftly, the man looked away. 'In February of this year, our Emperor issued the following edict - Nemo se hostiis polluat. This outlaws blood sacrifices. It forbids state officials to worship in a Pagan temple, or else they must face a heavy fine. My sources advise me that the next step could be to extinguish the eternal fire in the Temple of Vesta in Rome. Therefore, the Vestal Virgins would be disbanded. Taking the auspices will be punished – that is, men who consider the flights of birds to provide omens will no longer be tolerated. Practicing witchcraft will be punished. Ultimately, it is thought that no one shall be allowed to go to sanctuaries, walk through temples, or raise his eyes to statues created by the labour of man.'

Marcus couldn't help himself. All thoughts of Janus' disapproval of his relationship with Aemelia fled his mind. He shot a look at Janus, and saw his friend staring straight back at him. All the men, he would wager, were thinking the same thing - what would happen to the Mithraic Temple? To Coventina's Well? And even the Shrine to the Water Nymphs? To all the shrines to the domestic gods the villagers worshipped, and to the gods the soldiers worshipped in the fort?

The voice of the Commandant droned on about how he believed the Batavians were sensible men, they would not disappoint him in adopting these practices should it become law; and how he trusted the men to deal with the buildings and artefacts in an appropriate way if the occasion demanded it. All Marcus could think about, was his initiation to Nymphus tonight. What would happen then? He would have to put his trust in the Pater and in Mithras himself. It was all he could do.

After the meeting, the men filed away and Janus sought Marcus out.

His shock had given way to fury and his dark eyes blazed with anger and hatred. 'What do you understand about this decree?' spat out Janus. 'Do you feel the way I do, and the way the rest of the men do?' Marcus nodded.

'I do. It is despicable. We are peaceful men, here. We worship our gods quietly. There is no harm in what we do,' he said.

Janus threw his sword down with a clatter and glared at it, as if the sword had been responsible for the decree instead of Theodosius.'I wonder, does the good Commandant realise he named his beloved daughter after one of the most notorious Vestal Virgins?' Janus said, still glaring at his sword. 'Ha! Does he not realise she was executed four hundred years ago for having sexual intercourse?' He looked at Marcus. 'How would he feel if history repeated itself, I wonder?'

Marcus flushed. 'I'm sure that won't be an issue,' he said coldly. 'And are you aware that you are named after the two headed god, also known as Chaos? Whatever you may think, I am more concerned about the cult than dead Vestal Virgins. Perhaps I can find out some information tonight. I have a feeling they will not abandon the temple as easily as the Commandant anticipates.'

'"They"?' asked Janus. 'Should that not be "we"? "We" shall not abandon the temple easily? You are a part of it, are you not? You are going to be initiated to nymphus tonight, are you not?'

'Yes. "We". I meant "we", you know I did,' replied Marcus. 'Now, please excuse me. I need to get ready. I have much to do before sunset. I expect the Pater will have some advice tonight for us.'

He nodded a brief farewell to Janus and headed back to his quarters. Janus was his friend, but at times he felt as if he didn't know him very well. The flashes of temper he was wont to display were not one of his best traits.

'Understand that my name also reflects the patron of civil and social order!' called Janus after him. 'And unlike some, the god Janus does not have to watch his back!'

Marcus raised his hand in acknowledgement, but did not turn back to face him. He hoped that his friend would be sensible, and not do anything to sabotage either his position or the worship of the neighbourhood gods. He suppressed his own anger at the insinuations Janus had also made. What he and Aemelia did or did not do, were nobody's business but their own. He hadn't really thought about the fact she was named after that particular Vestal Virgin, though. And despite everything else, that image did bring rather an inappropriate smile to his lips.

# AD 391

Once more, Marcus lay blindfolded on the floor of the temple, his arms and legs stretched out like rays. He knew what to expect this time. But at least this time, he was partially clothed. He wore the loincloth of the Corax, but the stone flags were still bitter. He had gone past feeling simply cold; his hands and feet were numb, the chill spreading throughout the rest of his body. His face was pressed against the stone flags again. He could hear the Pater approaching the altar, the steady thump, thump, thump of his staff as he walked to the front of the temple.  The other members of the cult were reciting the sacred words as he passed them, the low hum of the chant filling the temple.

Marcus felt the swish of the Pater's robes as he came to stand before him and heard the Heliodromus move to the side.

'Welcome, faithful servants of Mithras. Today we have heard some disturbing news. Our beloved Emperor, Theodosius, has made some changes. Our beloved Commandant, Titus Perpetuus, chose to share those changes with us, and perhaps give us some idea of the future edicts that we will be forced to deal with.' There was an angry murmuring in the temple. Marcus shifted slightly. He wished the Pater would save the eulogising for later and initiate him. He was anxious to be done with the ceremony today. There was too much to think about. He hadn't seen Aemelia since the announcement and he was still angry with Janus. And the floor wasn't becoming any more comfortable, the longer he lay there.

The Pater continued,'We have also an initiation taking place tonight.' Marcus felt a slight pressure on his cheek. The Pater was nudging him with his toe. 'Corax Marcus Simplicius Simplex. Tonight you shall be initiated into the role of nymphus. This initiation has been delayed. You are overdue your promotion, Corax. It has been noted that you did not attend the previous ceremony. It has also been noted as to the reason why this occurred. The cult members watch and report, Corax. Should you not be willing to embrace our values and beliefs, you shall be suitably discharged from the service of Mithras.'

The murmuring in the temple changed to noises of assent.

'No third chances!' called someone. Marcus squirmed on the stone flags. He understood their annoyance with him, he really did. But he was here now. It was only one transgression.

'And may I also remind you of the vow of secrecy,' said the Pater. 'Our cult and our temple are sacrosanct, accessible only to the chosen few. Women are not allowed in the temple. Our beliefs are not to be discussed outside the temple. Our rituals are private.'

Marcus felt his cheeks flare in embarrassment and contrition. Had he really been so open about the temple? He could not think. He had spoken only to Janus. Yet who else may have heard the things he told them?

'So, on the understanding that you accept and embrace your duties, I shall commence the initiation. Please remember all I have told you tonight. Secrecy is paramount. Nothing which occurs here tonight may be discussed outside the temple. Do you understand, Corax?'

'Yes, Pater,' said Marcus, his voice muffled by the floor.

'Speak up,' commanded the Pater. 'We did not hear you.'

'Yes Pater!' shouted Marcus, raising his head painfully.

'Good. Now I shall begin,' said the Pater. Marcus knew the man was in charge here, but he could not help feeling the Pater was being a little overdramatic. He had hardly uncloaked the cult members and subsequently paraded them through the fort and the vicus, had he? He frowned beneath the blindfold and flexed his fingers. I must lose this attitude, he told himself. This is what I want. A picture of Janus' eager face flitted before his mind's eye, and he knew his friend longed to be in the position he was within the temple. Then just as quickly, an image of Janus' angry, contorted face flashed before him. He hoped that Janus wanted to join the cult for the right reasons. Any more thoughts such as these were chased from his mind as he heard the Pater begin the words of initiation he had first used when Marcus became a Corax.

'As the sun spirals its longest dance, cleanse your servant. As nature shows bounty and fertility, bless your servant. Let your servant live with the true intent of Mithras and enable him to fulfil his destiny. Marcus Simplicius Simplex, arise from the rock as our god Mithras was born from the rock. Let us witness the Slaying of the Bull.'

Marcus stood up, swaying slightly as the blood rushed back into his limbs. The Slaying of the Bull. It was the Water Miracle he had performed last time. This, then, was his next challenge. The low chanting began again, and he felt two men grasp his wrists and lead him to the side of the temple. This time, they did not bind him, but he felt something being placed into his hands. By the size and feel of the item, he realised it was a gladius – a sword.  He heard the door of the temple open and the chanting became louder and more insistent. There was a scuffling noise as they brought something in, and Marcus weighed the gladius in his hands. He knew how to wield these things to do the most damage. It was basic training for all legionaries. Swung from right to left, a gladius could decapitate a man. Brought straight down on the enemy's head, the sword would split it in two like a piece of fruit. He guessed they had found a wild animal. Or maybe one brought in one the domestic ones from the vicus or the fort. They are deliberately flaunting the edict banning blood sacrifice, Marcus thought. They will not accept these edicts as willingly as the Commandant hoped. His stomach flipped a little, realising that the further into the cult he went, the more militant he would be expected to become. Marcus was at heart a peaceful, quiet man. He had joined the army to protect the country and the people, not to instigate death and destruction.

'You understand what you hold in your hands, Corax Marcus Simplicius Simplex?' asked the Pater. Marcus nodded, then realised he was probably expected to speak.

'Yes, Pater. I am holding a gladius,' he said loudly and clearly. It echoed around the temple, his voice magnified, bouncing off the walls.

'You understand your foolish behaviour of the past?'

'Yes, Pater.'

'You understand that women should not be brought into the temple?'

'Yes, Pater.'

'You renounce your ill-advised judgement in these matters that have gone before us?'

'Yes, Pater.' Marcus' voice wavered a little. He didn't quite understand where this was leading to.

'You renounce Christianity and all that goes with it?'

There was a beat.

'Yes, Pater,' said Marcus, his voice guarded.

'All that goes with Christianity?' repeated the Pater.

'I...I do not understand, Pater?' asked Marcus. 'In what respect?'

'Exactly as I say. All that goes with Christianity. The belief system. The worship of one God. The people who subscribe to this religion.'

'I cannot do that, Pater,' said Marcus softly.

'I ask you once more,' said the Pater. 'The people who subscribe to this religion. Do you renounce them?'

'I cannot renounce them all, Pater,' said Marcus. His stomach was churning now. He would never do that. He could not renounce Aemelia for the sake of this cult.

'I have tried,' sighed the Pater. 'Yet I find it in my heart to continue the initiation. Mithras has willed it. But you must exercise better judgement, Corax Marcus, in all aspects of Mithraism. You have one more chance. Then you must face the consequences.'

'Yes, Pater,' replied Marcus. He made a mental note to give thanks to Mithras and Coventina when this was over. He would never bring Aemelia down here again. It was a small price to pay.

'To be initiated into the role of nymphus, you must perform the slaying. My Sun Runners will guide you to the centre of the temple. You must slay this animal, as Mithras slayed the sacred bull,' said the Pater.

Marcus was guided silently into the centre of the aisle and there were more scuffles and scrapes. The animal was trying to escape. They must have drugged it or silenced it somehow; there was no noise from the animal, apart from a guttural moan that went on and on and on. Marcus determined to complete the ritual quickly. He had seen animals sacrificed before; brought to their knees then slaughtered. It would be done cleanly.

'Corax Marcus Simplicius Simplex, slay the sacred bull!' bellowed the Pater.

Marcus roared, shouting a battle cry as he charged blindfolded towards the sacrifice. He felt the blade of the gladius sink into soft flesh, then force its way into bone. He heard a gurgling sound in the animal's throat, and pulled the blade out. He swung the sword to the right and yelled again as he brought it the blade crashing through where he visualised the animal's head to be. The gladius connected with something, then sliced through bone. Marcus knew if he hadn't decapitated the animal, he would at least have taken a piece of its skull away. There was a soft thud as the animal crumpled to the ground.

He waited for the cult members to resume their chanting as he completed his initiation, but there was a silence in the temple. Something warm and sticky ran over his foot and he could smell blood.

'Congratulations. You are now a nymphus. A sacred bridegroom,' said the Pater. His voice was soft and dangerous. There was a triumphant edge to it. 'Remove the bridegroom's blindfold, heliodromus.'

Someone pulled the blindfold off Marcus, and he blinked, his eyes watering. The candelight flickered in the temple and threw shadows over the bloodied heap, covered in a robe of some sort, in front of the altar. Marcus leaned over it to see what he had achieved.

'What – what is it?' he asked. It was too small to be a boar or a deer, or indeed any animal he had witnessed in the area. His eyes flicked across the temple to see where the head was. He hadn't managed to decapitate it. He had taken a slice off its skull. Blood and brain matter clung to the dark, curly hair on the piece of skull. Marcus suddenly retched. He ran back to the body in front of the altar.

'No. Please, no!' he cried. He ripped the robes off the body, dreading what he knew he would see beneath it. A deep gash gaped where his blade had pierced the chest. He grabbed the hand and saw the delicate gold ring on the little finger. He brought the smooth, white hand up to his face and closed his eyes. The floor felt as if it was shifting sand beneath his feet and there was a humming in his ears. Marcus cupped the bloodied, spoiled, face in his hands and stared at, willing this all to be a bad dream. Had it just been this afternoon when he had stroked that face in the garden? When he had kissed her? Her dark, unseeing eyes seemed to look straight into his soul. There was an expression of shock and disbelief on the girl's face. Marcus knew it was an image he would hold in his memory forever. It would never leave him.

'Aemelia!' he sobbed. 'Aemelia. May the gods forgive me! What did they make me do?' Then, with another battle cry, he leaped to his feet and swung around to face the cult members, grasping the gladius in both hands.

But the temple was empty. The cult members had been ushered out and the door barricaded, trapping Marcus inside. He ran at the door, screaming and stabbing it again and again, breaking it down splinter by splinter until he could escape.

By the time he pushed through the broken planks, it was pitch black outside and the countryside was deserted. He could hear the night-time noises carrying down the hill from the temple and the vicus settling down for the evening. He heard laughs and shouts coming from the taverns and brothels as people went home. Marcus collapsed on the ground outside the temple and lay on the grass, too numb to move or think. It began to snow, soft flakes at first, falling from the night sky. The snow came down harder and harder, covering everything with white. Marcus wanted to stay there, to die like Aemelia had, to be with her again in whatever afterlife they could meet in.

Marcus didn't know how long he had lain there, but someone walked past him and leaned over him. He thought they asked how he was and what had happened; but he didn't answer. He willed them to go away and leave him alone. The person knelt down beside him and touched his shoulder, but he flinched away. The person eased him up and wrapped their cloak around him. Then they began to guide him away from the temple. Marcus struggled, but the other person was stronger. They forced Marcus to put one foot in front of the other and returned with him to the fort. They took him back to his quarters and guided him into his bed. Then they sat with him until he eventually slept.

Marcus thought the person might have been Janus; but he wasn't sure. It could have been Janus. He might have been visiting Aelia.

# AD 391

Marcus was confined to his quarters for two days, as he burnt with a fever and rambled nonsense. On the third day, he managed to crawl out of bed and take his place in the ranks. His face was taut and pale, his eyes dull and blank. He was slow and uncoordinated, refusing to handle the gladius, preferring to supervise the legionaries instead. Janus came over to him after drill and took him behind the stable block.

'I have managed to explain your absence to the troops, and to keep people away from your quarters. I do not know what happened to you in the temple, but you can discuss it with me if you see it fit,' he said, his eyes searching Marcus' face for an answer. Marcus did not respond. He shook his head and pushed Janus out of the way, trying to get back to the quadrant.

'Marcus, my friend! What is the problem? Have I done anything to upset you in any way?' asked Janus, his face falling. 'What I said about Antonia, perhaps...' He looked askance at Marcus, half-smiling, trying to get him to acknowledge the deliberate mistake. It had become part of their banter, an accepted form of repartee.

'Don't,' said Marcus. He pressed his lips together and tried again to leave, pushing Janus out of the way.

'Marcus, this is madness. You have to tell me what has happened. There are rumours that your beloved has flown the coop. The Commandant has half the cohort searching for her in the countryside. Do you know anything...'

Before Janus could finish his sentence, Marcus turned and threw a punch at him. Janus ducked out of the way, an expression of disbelief on his face. He grabbed Marcus' wrist and twisted his arm behind him, making Marcus drop to the floor and cry out in pain.

'You are mad!' Janus cried, his eyes wide. He released his friend. 'Please. You have to tell me what happened. This is out of character for you.'

'I cannot tell you what happened!' hissed Marcus. 'It will put us both at risk. Just leave me alone!'

'I can help!' said Janus. 'You have to trust me. I know it has something to do with that girl. Please.'

Marcus sank down onto his haunches and dropped his head into his hands. He shook his head wordlessly and then covered his face. 'You cannot help. There is nothing you can do for me. This is my problem. Everything that happened was because of my mistakes. I cannot drag you into it,' he said, his voice cracking. 'Please. Just go back to the quadrant and leave me here. I shall follow later.'

Janus stood for a moment and stared down at Marcus. 'As you wish,' he said. 'But you can confide in me. Nothing about that cult can be that secretive. Nobody can be harmed by its actions.'

Again Marcus shook his head. 'You do not know the half of it,' he said. 'Leave me alone.'

Janus waited a moment more, then nodded. He turned and left Marcus and walked back towards the quadrant, his leather sandals wet from the slush that still lay on the ground.

Marcus stayed hidden behind the stable block for quite some time. The thought of going back into the company of the men made him feel physically sick. How many of them had witnessed the deed in the temple? How many of them knew the secret he had been sworn to keep? Everywhere he went, he felt as if eyes were staring at him, accusing him of the cold-blooded murder of an innocent girl. Every time he closed his eyes, the vision of her broken body lying in the temple haunted him. He couldn't share this with anyone; he just couldn't. It was a burden he would carry to the grave. Perhaps the search party would give up; perhaps her body would have been disposed of somehow and nobody need know what had happened. Perhaps some merciful battle would occur and he would be killed by the Barbarians, and no longer have to suffer...

Marcus hauled himself up from the ground and made his way slowly back to the quadrant. He pulled up short as a flurry of activity blurred before his eyes. Men were running around, not in the neat ranks they were used to, but scurrying back and forth, casting terrified glances at one another. He stood motionless as the Commandant and his wife appeared from their home, surrounded by guards. The Commandant had aged over the last few days; his wife was being supported by another woman as she wept hysterically. Someone ran up to him and grasped his arm.

'They found the girl!' said the man. Marcus registered that it was Felix. 'Or what was left of her. They found her body hidden on the moors! She's been murdered. They tried to decapitate her.' Marcus blanched and felt himself sway. He steadied himself by clutching Felix.

'When?' he asked, fighting back the nausea he felt rising from his stomach into the back of his throat.

'Not long ago. They brought her back. The Commandant is going to make us pay for this. It's not fair! We are all honest men here. Who would harm a girl like that?'

'I do not know,' said Marcus. He stared across at the gathering troops. The Commandant was searching the men for a guilty face. The sweat beaded on Marcus' brow. He would sense it. Titus Perpetuus would know who was to blame. Slowly, he took his place in the line, trying to compose his features and maintain a blank expression.

When everyone was silent, the Commandant stood on the plinth and faced the men.

'Cohort!' he bellowed. 'You know why I have gathered you together. My daughter has been savagely murdered and I believe the culprit is standing in this square.' His face worked as his voice caught on the words. His wife collapsed into the arms of her slave and howled in despair. 'I shall stop at nothing to find the guilty party,' continued the Commandant. 'Somebody here knows something about it. You have twenty four hours to do the honourable thing and confess your part in the attack. Should you not confess, I shall begin the most savage punishment available to me as a Commandant. I shall order decimation, until somebody confesses to this crime.'

There was an audible gasp from the soldiers. They had heard of this punishment, but it had never been carried out within this cohort. One man in every ten would be randomly slaughtered. They all looked at one another, terrified. To be killed honourably in battle was one thing. To be killed by your own men, by your friends and colleagues was horrific.

'The gates to the fort will be barricaded until this matter is resolved: in either way. Dismissed!' stated the Commandant and turned his back on the cohort. Placing his arm around his wife, he guided her back into their home. A slave closed the door behind them and the quadrant erupted.

'Who is responsible for this?' cried one of the Centurions. 'You must confess. We are all at risk because of you!' The men echoed his cry and the men turned to one another, scanning the troops, looking – as the Commandant had looked – for a guilty man.

'You were the last person to see her,' said someone. Marcus stared at the man who had spoken. It was Milenius, the standard bearer. 'What happened after you left her? We saw you leaving Aelia's garden together. Longinius and I were in the market,' Marcus shook his head mutely. 'Speak to us!' said Milenius. 'Tell us what happened.' His face was hard, suspicious.

'She...she was alive,' Marcus managed. 'I came back to the fort. I...'

'And what happened after that?' pressed Milenius. 'Did you see her any more that evening? We have to piece it together. If you are innocent, you have to give us all the information.' His eyes roved around the quadrant. 'These men; your friends. Your troops. We are all at risk. We must work together to solve this.'

'A Barbarian,' stammered Marcus. 'Or – or a Pict. They came to the defences; maybe took her away...?'

Milenius looked at him in disbelief. 'Do not treat us as if we are uneducated idiots,' he said. 'You know that could not have happened. Carrawburgh is guarded at all times.'

'Then I cannot help you,' said Marcus. He turned away from the standard bearer and pushed his way through the anxious men who were shouting theories at one another in panic. This whole episode was a disaster. Marcus could see no resolution to it. He hurried away towards his quarters. Perhaps he could lock himself in there and pray to the gods, for what it would be worth, anyway.

'Marcus!' He heard a voice calling after him. He began to run faster. Yet he knew in his heart he would look like a guilty man by running. Perhaps they would misinterpret it; they might think that he had realised he would be one of the Prefects chosen to carry out the decimation. 'Marcus!' Footsteps pounded up behind him. It was Janus again. Of course. The man missed nothing.

'I told you, leave me alone,' said Marcus.

'No. You know more than I think you do,' said Janus. 'Does it have something to do with the cult? That is the only thing you can be hiding from me.'

'I can't tell you!' shouted Marcus.

'Yes, you can,' said Janus coldly. 'It has to be the cult. Look. I shall make it easy for you. I can maybe help you. But you have to trust me. You have to tell me exactly what happened in the temple. If you feel you can do this, I shall be waiting for you behind the bath house at midnight. Then we can decide what to do. If not. Well,' he shrugged, defeated. 'I shall see you tomorrow, and we shall take turns killing innocent men. Perhaps you will have to kill me. Or I you. Think about it, Marcus. You can prevent it, if you share the secret with me.'

Marcus twisted around and looked at Janus. He shook his head slightly, then turned away, leaving Janus standing at the edge of the building watching him as he disappeared into his quarters.

Marcus sat on his bed rocking to and fro, trying to decide what to do. The orders of the Pater resounded in his head – Secrecy is paramount. Nothing which occurs here tonight may be discussed outside the temple. He grasped the edge of the mattress and stared at the door to his room. The remains of a small fire smouldered in the grate and as he focussed on the dying flames he knew had to make a choice. He could not let innocent men suffer because of his mistakes. Had he known the power of the cult, he would have stayed away from it. He could not let Janus make the same mistake.

He had to tell him what had happened. Then he would confess to the Commandant, explain what had happened. He knew he could face execution himself for his part in the tragedy; but if it would save the men, he would take the chance. He looked around his room, wondering if tonight would be the last time he slept in it. Then he stood up and pushed the door open. He would meet Janus at midnight as he had requested and tell him the truth.

# 1650

'Did you miss me, Meggie?' asked Charles Hay. He was lurking in the alleyway beside her house, waiting for her to come back home. She had been to the Well, praying to Coventina. She had slipped out in the early hours before dawn, terrified that someone might see her and taunt her. They were calling her a murderess and only yesterday she had found a hen, its neck twisted and broken, lying outside of her cottage.

'Mr Hay!' Meggie said, stopping short. He came out of the shadows, grasping his ever-present whip. Meggie heard his horse whinnying softly behind the house. Charles stood between Meggie and the doorway to her home and smiled down at her. Meggie clutched her shawl to her body instinctively.

Hay saw the movement and his lips parted in amusement. 'Dear Meggie. What's wrong with you? Are you not pleased to see me again?' He pouted and tilted his head on one side. In anyone else, the gesture may have been appealing. In Charles Hay, it seemed more mocking. He raised his hand and touched her hair gently. His nose wrinkled and he drew his hand away. 'Ah Meggie.

THE MEMORY OF SNOW

If things were different, eh? If you came and lived at the Manor with me. Then you could have all the finery and delights a young woman could want. You would have hot water to wash with, enough food to fill your little belly. We'd get some meat on those bones nigh enough.' He sighed and looked at her worn dress and bare feet. 'Yes. Some dainty little kid slippers for those tiny feet and a frock made of silks and velvet. You'd be perfect. Nobody would know where you'd come from or how you'd been dragged up on these moors.' He stared into the middle distance thoughtfully and his horse gave a snort. Charles laughed and jerked his head towards the animal. 'Hear that, my Meg? Jessie agrees with me. You would have your own little pony to ride, just like her. She would take you off, clip-clopping to that Well you often visit…what? What's wrong? Don't you realise that I know where it is? I've followed you a few times, wondering where you were going. It's a special place to you, isn't it?'

Meggie hung her head, flushing scarlet. For a moment, she had been mesmerised by his voice, imagining all the things she might be if she didn't live the way she had to; if she didn't just simply exist in this village. She was nineteen years old. She had nobody on this earth who cared for her. A tear rolled down her cheek as she recalled Alice's face. Now even she was gone.

143

Meggie took a deep breath. 'Mr Hay, you are a cruel man,' she said softly. 'Please. Let me pass and enough of this conversation. I can never be anything more than what I am. I am indebted to you for the generous payments you make me, but that money is all I have. Please do not taunt me with a life I cannot live.'

She made to push past him, but he barred her way. 'Meggie, come on. It can be, you know. You only have to say the word,' he whispered, leaning down and bringing his lips close to her ear. She jerked her head away from him and tried once more to get past him, into the safety of her cottage. It was daybreak now, and people would soon be out of their homes. If they saw her talking to Charles, or even just saw her outside, there was no telling what might happen.

She began to panic as she heard a door further along the street creaking open and looked up at the young man pleadingly. 'I have to get in the house, I have to get in,' she said and summoning all her strength, roughly pushed him out of the way.

Charles stumbled and stared at her. 'Why Meggie, I didn't know you possessed such strength. By all means, go inside. I shall follow you in.'

'No!' she cried. 'Please. Go home.' She fumbled with the handle and eventually fell into the cottage, just as she heard a woman's voice calling to her friend down the road.

'It's a fine morning today!' the woman shouted. She saw Charles Hay look around him and slip into the cottage after Meggie.

The woman stood staring at the scene, and immediately jogged down the road to her friend. 'There must be another one in trouble,' she said. 'He's at her house again.'

'No, I don't think so,' said the second woman, shaking her head. 'I think he's going for a bit of fun with her instead. Lord knows she'll be willing to take anybody now and she'll be grateful for the attention. That's why she's been hiding away. I bet she's the one in trouble.'

'Yes. You'll be right. That's what it is. Typical,' replied the first woman, glaring at the ramshackle building. 'Well, she'll not keep a secret like that for long. There'll be one more brat coming squawling into the village, staring at us with Mr Hay's eyes, I'll warrant.'

The second woman nodded. 'Aye, there will be that,' she said.

Inside the cottage, Meggie laid her basket down on the stone floor. Silent as night, Charles closed the door behind him and stared at the girl before him.

'So. We're alone again,' he said.

Meggie spun round. 'You followed me!' she accused him.

'Of course I did! I said I would, Meg. I do not lie, you should know that by now.' Charles looked around the small room and his eyes lighted on a wooden stool by the hearth. 'Is that your only seat?' he asked. Meggie nodded, ashamed that he should be standing in her home. What would it look like through his eyes? Poky, no doubt. And dark and small. But it was warm, thanks to the fire she kept burning in the grate. It was as clean as she could keep it. She didn't have many possessions, so she took care of what she did have. Bunches of herbs hung from the beams in the ceiling and small earthenware jars containing ointments and tinctures stood on a scrubbed table by the window. A pestle and mortar lay beside them, together with a small, sharp knife she used for splitting the stems of the plants and chopping up leaves as she needed them; she had found it on the moors and it seemed perfect for her work. A wooden bowl full of lavender was Meggie's only ornament, the purple, knobbly flowers spilling out onto the windowsill.

'Mr Hay, I'm sure you are a very busy man, so unless there is anything you need me to do for you today, I'll bid you farewell,' said Meggie. She turned her back on him and began to lay some wood on the fire.

'Don't turn your back on me, Meggie,' said Charles. His voice was low. Meggie heard him take a step towards her and wait. She finished piling the wood onto the fire and waited until it began to crackle. She straightened up. Turning to face the young man, she waited in silence for his next comment, her heart banging against her chest.

He smiled at her. 'That's good, Meg. Now we can see each other properly. Be a sweetheart and open your curtains will you? Well, I think they are meant to be curtains. Or 'it' is meant to be a type of curtain. It looks like an old sack, really. But that can't be right. Anyway. As I say, be a sweetheart and pull it open. I want to see outside. It's such a beautiful morning.' He sat down on the stool, seeming to fill the tiny room with his presence. Meggie's heart began to race. All her instincts were screaming at her to run out of the house, and damn what the village would say to her. It was wrong him being in here. He didn't need her to do anything for him. Wordlessly, she went over to the window and twitched it open.

Meggie's house was right on the street. Anybody walking past could look into her cottage. And they did. Which is why she had nailed the curtain up above the window. Too many people had taken to stopping outside and staring into her house these last few weeks. Gaggles of villagers would congregate there and she could see their lips moving and their heads nodding towards her house, bobbing around to see if they could see her and see what she was doing. Perhaps she was concocting another murderous potion, who knew? Lizzie had often been amongst the women, nodding along with them. She had been there the day Meggie scrambled up on the table and battered the nails into the window frame to pin the sack in place. Meggie had caught her eye. Lizzie dropped her head and tucked a stray strand of hair behind her ear. Lizzie's youngest, a baby boy was grizzling as he hung over her shoulder, his cheeks flushed red. He had one tiny fist rammed into his mouth and he was chewing on it desperately. Meggie longed to offer Lizzie something to soothe the baby's gums until his pearly teeth cut through them. Meggie had done it for Lizzie's other two children. In fact, she had done it for most of the children in the village. How quickly people forgot. Instead, she had pulled the sacking straight and clambered down off the table, leaving Lizzie and her crones outside with nothing to stare at except brown hessian. Meggie had sat on the floor, hugging her knees. She laid her head on them and cried; although nobody heard her and nobody cared enough to soothe her pain.

'That's better,' said Charles. His voice brought her back to the present. She turned around, her hand behind her back, leaning on the table.

'You realise that everyone can look into the room now? You know that you will be seen, don't you?' she said. Charles nodded.

'I do. That does not concern me. I don't have to live in the village,' he said. Meggie shuddered. He was right, of course. Whatever he had in mind did not bother him in the slightest. 'Now, Meggie, come here,' he continued. 'I would like to speak to you.'

'What do you want with me, Mr Hay?' she asked.

'Now, now. Come closer. Don't stand over there, my sweet Meg. You know of course that I've been in Newcastle these last few days, don't you? It seems as if I have missed quite a lot in the village. It all stems back to Alice. It was Alice, wasn't it?' For a moment his expression was blank, as if he was trying to remember the girl who had died. 'Yes, that's right. Alice.' He sighed. 'Poor girl. Never mind. What is done cannot be undone and we must leave her to rest in peace. So. That leaves you. It appears to me that you seem to be shouldering the blame for this. On such dear, fragile, little shoulders.' He reached out and touched Meggie on the shoulder, the cloth of her gown rough against his fingers. He took a corner of the fabric between his thumb and forefinger and rubbed it together. 'Silks and velvet, my dear Meggie. Silks and velvet. I could do that for you. But there would have to be certain compromises. Do you understand me?'

Meggie stood before him in silence. Was this the same offer he had made to other girls in the village? Made them promises he had no intention of keeping, just to satisfy him for a moment in his spoiled, rich life? Meggie had never hated anyone before. She had disliked Charles' actions in the past, but she had tolerated him. It is what the gentry do, her Grandmother had told her. Do their bidding and take their payments. This is our gift. Use it well and use it to your advantage. And always use it wisely.

Charles ran his fingers over the seams of her gown and down her arms.

'Please, Mr Hay. Don't do this,' said Meggie.

'Don't do what?' he asked innocently. 'This? Do you not like it?' he said. He took hold of her arms and stood up, staring down at Meggie. His fingers dug into the soft flesh of her arms and he drew her closer to him. He took hold of her around her waist and lowered his head. He brushed his lips against her forehead. Then he travelled down to her neck.

'Mr Hay...' said Meggie, trying to pull away from him. 'No. No. I don't want to do this, it's wrong.'

'Alice didn't think it was wrong,' said Charles. 'Alice liked it. She liked it very much. She-argh!' He screamed as the sharp blade of the knife stabbed into the flesh between his shoulder blades. 'What the hell did you do?' he screamed, trying to feel around behind his shoulders. The blade was too small to do much damage, but it had drawn blood and this was now running down Charles' back in a warm, sticky rivulet. He brought his hands around to the front and stared at them as the red stuff dripped onto his clothing. 'You are mad!' he said, horrified. 'Completely mad.'

'You shouldn't speak of Alice like that,' hissed Meggie. 'Never speak of her like that.' She held the knife in front of her; she had snatched it from the table beside the window as she leaned against it. 'You raped Alice. She told me. Don't you dare speak of her as if she enjoyed it!'

Charles lunged towards Meggie and she ducked out of his way.

She brandished the knife again. 'Take one step closer,' she growled. 'One more step. And I shall do it again. Only this it will be in your neck. Or your eye. Or your heart.'

Charles hesitated for a minute, then turned and lurched out of the cottage. He spilled out on the street, blinking in the bright sunlight which had now settled over the village. The back of his shirt was stained red and his back was throbbing painfully. Each pump of his heart seemed to spurt a little more of his blood out. He needed to get home. He needed the doctor. But how could he explain this to his father? The ubiquitous gaggle of women had already gathered in the street, gratified that Meggie had pulled the curtain down and they could see inside her cottage once more. Unfortunately, nobody had seen exactly what had happened with Charles. They had only seen him bursting out of the cottage with blood running down his back and a terrified expression on his face.

'Mr Hay, Sir!' cried Mary, a woman in her late forties who refused to believe that she simply was not as attractive as the younger females in the village. 'What happened? What did she do to you?'

Charles glared at the woman; he recognised her vaguely from his sojourns in the village and tired easily of her sniffing around him. He would never bed her; never. And now she was poking her pock-marked nose in where it did not belong. Normally, he would not even speak to a woman such as her. But today, he would make an exception.

'She is mad!' he stated. 'Completely and utterly mad. I went to sympathise over the loss of her friend, and she turned on me. Just turned on me. She stabbed me. She enticed me in and then stabbed me!'

The gaggle of women cried out in shock. The girl had finally turned. She was a danger to everyone now. She was attacking people at random.

'Mr Hay, you shouldn't have gone in! She's a witch! She knows what to do to entice people in to her. Then she kills them, like she did with poor Alice! You've had a lucky escape, Mr Hay. A lucky escape indeed. Do you need to rest, Sir? I can let you have a seat in my house?' said Mary, hardly daring to believe her chance may have finally come. 'I have a warm bed, Sir. You could lay down in it and regain your strength?'

But Charles did not respond. He turned his back on the women and limped through the alleyway to where Jess was waiting for him, chewing her way through the grass at the side of the track out of the village.

'She is an enchantrix,' muttered Charles, repeating a comment he'd heard in Newcastle. He mounted his horse and galloped off to the manor house, kicking her flanks and making her speed across the moors before the pain in his back became too unbearable.

The women looked at each other.

'What's an enchantrix?' asked Mary. The others shrugged. They had no idea. Lizzie thought she knew. She also thought that she knew what had happened in Meggie's cottage that morning. But she said nothing. Instead, she hoisted her mewling baby onto her shoulders and peeled away from the group, taking one last look back at the cottage. Meggie had wasted no time. The sackcloth was back in place, blocking her home from the outside world. She was already lighting a smudge stick made of sage leaves to cleanse and purify her house after Hay had defiled it.

# AD 391

It was cold outside, the temperature dropping and the slushy snow from a few days beforehand freezing over. The moon was a huge silver disc hanging low in the sky, lighting the path through the fort towards the bath house.

When Marcus turned the corner behind the building, a dark shadow broke away from the wall and a solid figure blocked his path.

'You came, then,' said Janus. 'I thought you would.'

'I had to,' said Marcus. 'I could not let the Commandant punish my men for a crime none of them committed. I have already decided what to do.' He shivered, but whether it was from fear or cold, even Marcus himself did not know.

'Are you going to tell him the truth?' asked Janus.

Marcus took a deep breath.'I am. And before I speak to the Commandant, I needed to speak to you, my friend. You need to understand what these people are capable of.'

'I am listening,' said Janus. 'Please. I would like to know what happened. Am I correct in assuming that this involves the followers of Mithras?'

Again, Marcus nodded, his shoulders sagging. 'It does. I shall be brief. I went to the temple to be initiated to the next rank within the cult. I missed the first date they provided me with, so they decreed another.'

'Why did you miss the first date?' asked Janus. 'It is so important to check these things, to see the information they offer you, surely?'

'I missed it because of Aemelia,' said Marcus. 'I had taken her down there, and I did not go in as I should have done.'

'Hmmm. It was an auspicious day, was it not?' asked Janus.

'Yes. I should have gone in, or at least returned later. But I did not.'

'Women are not allowed in the temple,' stated Janus. 'I thought you would have adhered to that rule. You should not have taken her there.'

'I know,' said Marcus. He sat down on a stone bench outside the bath house and leaned his head against the wall, closing his eyes in defeat. 'Then I went with you. And that was the day I had to return; I was to be initiated that night.'

'How fortuitous, then, that I made you go,' said Janus, sitting next to him. 'You would have missed that date as well.'

'So I returned for the initiation,' continued Marcus. 'And I lay on the floor until the Pater came in. Then he asked me to renounce all things

Christian. I would not. I could not renounce her. So they told me I had to perform the sacrificial ritual. And I did. But it was her, Janus. I killed Aemelia. I stabbed her and I sliced her skull open with the gladius.' His voice broke and he shuddered, remembering it all too clearly.

'Ah, Marcus,' sighed Janus. He put his arm around his shoulders and squeezed. 'What a situation.'

'I know,' replied Marcus. He dropped his head and covered his face with his hands. 'I wanted to let you know before you joined the cult. To save you from being involved. Janus, how can I tell her father that I killed her? It is too dreadful to contemplate.'

'You do not have to,' said Janus. 'I shall take care of that issue for you.' He pulled Marcus closer to him and, leaning towards his ear, dropped his voice to a whisper. 'Can you remember what the Pater told you, my friend? "Secrecy is paramount. Nothing which occurs here tonight may be discussed outside the temple. Our rituals are private". How soon you forget. You forget also that, should you not be willing to embrace our values and beliefs, you shall be suitably discharged from the service of Mithras. There are no third chances, Corax. Or should I say nymphus. You did achieve the sacrifice, after all. You have used up your last chance. Now you must face the consequences. The Pater must deal with this disgrace and silence you.'

'What?' cried Marcus. 'Janus…' But the man's hand came around his mouth swiftly and blocked any noise he could have made. Marcus began to feel dizzy as the pieces tumbled into place. He tried to struggle free, his eyes wide and horrified. This was the ultimate betrayal. Janus had known about his initiation before he did – he knew he was going to be made a nymphus. He had blurted it out that time he lost his temper: and Marcus, equally heated, had not realised. Janus knew about the wax tablet system. Marcus was willing to bet it was not by accident he had asked him to go to the temple with him that fateful day. A dozen other little incidents slipped into place – the encouragement to discuss the rituals, the pressing questions. It was all a test. A test that he had finally failed.

Marcus felt the sharp blade of a knife pressing up against his throat as Janus twisted his head around. He began to panic, ragged breath escaping as he strove in vain to free himself. But Janus held him fast. He was a Prefect in the Roman Army. A trained killer.

'As the sun spirals its longest dance, cleanse your servant,' whispered Janus. 'As nature shows bounty and fertility, bless your servant. Let your servant live with the true intent of Mithras, serving him until death...'

The last conscious thought that Marcus had before the lethal blade severed his artery, was of Aemelia.

# 1650

'Hear ye, hear ye! All people that would bring in any complaint against any woman for a witch, they should be sent for and tried by the person appointed!'

The crier rode ahead of the entourage. A man dressed in black sat on a pure white horse, flanked by guards who had sworn to protect him and bring him safe passage through the borders. This small village was on the English side of the border, to the west of Newcastle. Cuthbert Nicholson was anxious to visit the place, having met some members of the Hay family whilst he was working in Newcastle. He felt assured of a night's rest and a good meal with the family. And if he could prove his worth in the village, it would be a coup for him as well.

'Hear ye! Hear ye! All people that would bring in any complaint against any woman for a witch, they should be sent for and tried by the person appointed!' repeated the crier. 'Hear ye! Hear ye!'

The villagers who straggled around the streets stared at the procession as it passed them. This must be the famous witch hunter they had heard about. Women looked at one another, assessing their neighbours, wondering whether they were harbouring a black secret.

'We are here to help you!' declared the crier, bringing his horse to a stop. 'This gentleman has been tasked with cleansing your village, ridding it from evil. If you have any complaints of this nature, tell us. The woman will have a fair trial and your minds will be settled!' He looked around the village, at the scrawny, unkempt women huddled beneath their shawls. He noted an elderly lady; the toothless, hunched woman, who went by the name of Agnes. He pointed at her. 'You. Do you practice the dark arts? Do you know of anyone in the village who practices them? You are obliged to tell us...'

'No!' cried Mary. She was Agnes' daughter and ran up to her mother, who was trembling with fear. 'My mother is a good, gentle, kindly woman. It is not the likes of her you need to be searching for.' Mary looked around at the crowd who were gathering around them. 'I think we all know who these gentlemen need to speak to.' Her face hardened and she clutched onto her mother's arm. 'We all know of someone who we could take to task for this.'

'Pray tell us, young lady,' said the crier. Mary was anything but a 'young lady', but his flattery worked. She preened herself, scooping her filthy, mousy-brown hair behind her shoulders and smiling at the man on horseback.

She flicked a glance at Nicholson. 'Is this gentleman here to be trusted?' she asked, suddenly brave. 'How can we be sure he knows what he is looking for?'

The crier smiled at her; a smile which did not reach his eyes but melted her guard a little more.

'My dear lady, you speak as if there is someone here who you do not trust. Tell me. Is this person a young woman herself?' He scanned the crowd. There were only a couple of elderly ladies in amongst them. Experience told him they were stalwarts of the village, central repositories of gossip. These women, unlike some in other areas, were not at risk of accusation. The hag's daughter, on the other hand, looked and acted like a whore; primping and preening herself, thrusting her breasts out unconsciously in his party's direction. He sensed competition for something here. A younger woman, perhaps, who was a threat to this female.

'Don't tell him anything!' A voice burst through the crowd. The crier looked around to see who had spoken. It was another woman, in her mid-twenties, perhaps? Two small children hung about her person and a baby squalled on her shoulder. 'Leave it be,' she said, addressing the whore. 'Don't do it.'

The crier ignored her. He spoke to the whore again. Tell me, my lady. Is this person a charmer?

An enchantrix, perhaps? Has this person proved this to you, over and over again?'

'Just the once that I know of,' said Mary. 'But she drew blood from the young master.'

'Of whom do you speak, when you talk of the 'young master'?' The man dressed in black spoke out clearly and his voice was mesmerising to the villagers.

'Why, Mr Hay, of course,' replied Mary.

'Mary...' said the dark haired girl. 'Stop it. You don't know where this is leading to.'

'You saw it Lizzie. You saw it as well as I did,' said Mary. She was not going to let Meggie get away with that. 'The poor young man, he only went to see her to tell her he was sorry about her friend passing like she did. And she stabbed him. She did, she stabbed him!' said Mary, passionate now.

'You've only got his story,' said Lizzie. 'You don't know...'

'Silence!' It was the dark man on the white horse who spoke to them. 'I am a personal friend of young Mr Hay. Who is this girl? As my good friend here asked you; is she a suspected charmer? An enchantrix? A witch, perhaps? Did she lure him into her cottage with tales of woe and bewitch the poor man?'

'We don't know that!' said Lizzie, looking frantically about her. There was that word again –

enchantrix. Her sister had told her it had something to do with witches. They lured men in and they charmed them. This is what they were accusing Meggie of. If they arrested Meggie, she would tell them about Lizzie and everyone would know. They would talk about her. The woman who had carried Hay's bastard child. Look at her, they would say. Her husband dead less than a twelve month. Lizzie was ashamed of herself. Hay had come to her door, allegedly bringing his condolences; she guessed he had tried the same trick on Meggie. Only Lizzie had been weak. Then she had been forced to call on Meggie and beg for her help.

Nicholson stared at Lizzie, saw the terror in her face and considered for a moment. He would be interested in seeing this 'enchantrix' they talked about. If Hay had pursued her, she must be a good looking woman. Hay would not approach someone he felt was less than deserving of his attentions. He guessed the dark-haired woman had tales of her own to tell. But he would leave her alone for now. He would concentrate on this other girl. If that brought no joy, then he could move on to this Lizzie creature. He tried to imagine Lizzie naked as he probed her with the needle on the end of his staff in order to find a soft, clean spot to prick her. She would do as some gentle amusement, he thought, but he would let her go afterwards. Maybe do an extra test on her, so could watch her blood flow down her white shift, then he would declare her innocent. But he was intrigued by this other girl.

'Yes! What was that funny word you used, Sir? Enchant-something-or-other?' cried Mary.

'Enchantrix,' replied Nicholson, curling his lip with distaste as he looked at this stupid, ill-educated and over-confident wench.

'Yes. That's it. She's an enchantrix. Mr Hay said so when he was running away from her. He didn't want to be there with her, he was running like he was scared of her. Like he'd come to his senses,' declared Mary. She put her hands in her hips and nodded. 'Yes, Sir. I know what she is now. It makes sense. She does odd things, Sir. Has funny beliefs. I can tell you where she might be if you like? If she's not in her cottage there,' she nodded towards the little house with the sacking across the window, 'then she'll be up on the moors, doing weird stuff with herbs and the like. She was raving that she'd seen her friend's ghost up there. Mad, I tell you. Mad.'

'Or a witch,' replied Nicholson. 'Bell – find out from this woman where this witch practices the dark arts. We shall track her down and deal with her. Fret not, my dear,' he said, bowing to Lizzie, as a man broke away from the processions and dismounted from his horse to speak with Mary. 'The witch will be given a fair trial. We do not deal in false accusations. We strive to discover the truth.

Good day,' he said. He could practically feel the three pounds he would earn from this village in his leather purse. If he didn't get this enchantrix they were talking about, he would get one of the others. Either the dark-haired one, the hag or the whore. He didn't care which one. It would be more fun trying the younger ones though. He looked forward to the challenge.

# AD 391

'I request an audience with the Commandant,' stated Janus. He was standing at the door of the Commandant's house, his breath freezing in small puffs as he faced the man who served as a sort of porter to the Commandant. The man looked at him.

'What is it that you wish to discuss with him?' he asked.

'I have information relating to the murder of his daughter,' replied Janus. The porter nodded and closed the door. Janus waited silently, fingering the item he had brought with him. It had been almost too easy. The necklace had been simple to unclasp. The ring had slipped effortlessly off her finger as well; he knew Marcus had paid a good deal of money to have that made for her. The sentiment it portrayed was practically Christian. Janus grimaced in distaste. That was why he had disposed of the ring – he had thrown it in the back of a cart bound for Corstopitum. The less Christian artefacts around here, the better. Plus, if the Commandant ever saw it, it would be more difficult for his story to be believable.

After Janus had taken Marcus back to his quarters, he returned to the temple. The girls' body was still there. Janus knew that the cult members would not dare to return to deal with it. At heart, they were all peaceful men. He was still annoyed that he had been left with the clearing up; but the men needed to be taught a lesson. He was certain it would have worked. Secrecy was paramount, and most of the men had family in the fort or lovers in the vicus. Janus had removed the jewellery and slung Aemelia's body across his shoulders. He took it across the moors and rolled it into a disused quarry. He had returned to the temple afterwards and seen the skull. He had picked it up, and to his mild disgust it was still sticky with her blood. He had taken the skull to Coventina's Well and thrown it in. The water was deep enough; they would never drain it. It would stay there forever. The corner of his lip curled into a slight smile. It was quite ironic. The Christian girl had become a sacrifice and finally an offering to the Pagan gods. Then Janus had slipped back into Marcus' room and taken the tiny bone-handled knife from his quarters. Janus knew that it would come in useful. He hadn't risen to Pater by hesitating during moments like that. Then the rest happened just as smoothly as he had expected. He knew Marcus would come to find him wanting to confess to his sins. It was in his nature. Janus sighed. He would never have amounted to much in the cult; he obviously didn't have the dedication required. A few years ago, it wouldn't have mattered so much. But Emperor Theodosius had a lot to answer to; he was trying to turn the Empire Christian, to upset all the belief systems that had been in force for centuries. Janus knew it was because he was trying to keep Bishop Ambrose happy. But why should the entire Empire pay for Theodosius' mistakes? It wasn't their fault the Bishop had excommunicated him. Had they ordered that massacre he had been involved in? No. So why should they suffer?

His thoughts were interrupted as the porter opened the door to the quarters and beckoned him in.

'The Commandant will see you now. He wishes this matter to be resolved as quickly as possible,' said the porter. Janus nodded and followed the man through the villa and into the Commandant's private apartments. A small fountain trickled in the atrium. The icy conditions must not have affected that too much, thought Janus. He despaired of this place, he really did. Coventina was supposed to melt the snow and make the rivers run again. Perhaps the offering he had thrown into her Well had done some good after all.

# 1650

Meggie looked up at the sky and shivered. It was March, but the winter seemed to have lasted an age. A heavy, grey cloud was moving slowly through the leaden sky. She knew it would bring snow with it. Out here on the moor, there was nowhere to shelter. She would rather stay here, though, than go back home and face the villagers. Gossip had spread around the place like a worm – she was being accused of turning on 'poor Mr Hay' and attacking him for no reason. She had come out to Coventina's Well to try and ground herself; to find some inner peace and ask the goddess for guidance. She had almost come to the end of her money and she knew that she couldn't rely on Hay any more for an income. She was considering leaving the village and going to one of the bigger towns – like Hexham, or maybe Newcastle – and finding some sort of work there. She could go further if she needed to. She could just disappear, and nobody would bother her.

The first few flakes of snow fluttered down and Meggie pulled her shawl closer to her body. Her gaze drifted up to the old Roman fort and she saw the man again. She was used to him now; a dark human-shaped figure, standing on the side of the hill. A robe flapped around his body and he was holding a sword in his hand. He usually stayed there for a few moments then disappeared. Sometimes, she felt his presence beside her at the Well. He didn't scare her any more. The one person she longed to see was Alice. If she couldn't see her shade, then this man's was proof that something existed after death; and in some small way it gave her comfort.

But today, there was something different. Meggie cursed her poor eyesight and squinted into the snow flurry. The spectral soldier seemed to be raising his hand and he pointed it in her direction. From behind him, came more shapes. They broke away from their solid, black mass and separated out into a group of men. These were no Roman soldiers, Meggie realised. They were as human as she was. Their voices carried faintly down the hill on the wind and someone led a horse to the man at the front. He mounted it and began to walk it down the hillside, followed by a line of men on foot. Meggie watched as they snaked down the hillside and her heart began to pound. What did they want?

'You have to leave here,' said a voice. She jumped and looked around. There was nobody there.

'Who speaks?' she asked. 'Who are you?'

'It was a mistake,' the voice said. 'If you stay, you will suffer for your mistake as well. They lied.'

Meggie stood up and turned herself slowly in a circle, searching for the owner of the voice.

'Please, show yourself to me,' she said. 'Are you the soldier? Are you the spirit who haunts here? Or do you bring me a message from the deities of this sacred place?'

There was an almighty crack and one of the stones which surrounded the Well fractured from top to bottom. Meggie jumped backwards in shock.

'There have been too many mistakes!' said the voice. A hazy figure broke away from the shadows of the Well and stood before her. As he became stronger, his eyes burned into hers. They were a deep, cornflower blue and seemed to Meggie to hold indescribable suffering; she sensed a torment that was somehow keeping him tied to this place. She knew that this was the man she had seen looking across from Carrawburgh fort so often.

'What happened to you?' she whispered. 'I can help you. I have been trained ...'

The man shook his head. He looked past her, at the train of men approaching the Well.

'We are too late,' he said. Meggie turned and followed his gaze. She saw the men coming towards her and her mouth went dry. She looked back to where the man had been, but he had gone.

# AD 391

The porter bowed as he opened the door into the Commandant's room and stood aside to allow Janus to pass. Janus waited until he heard the door shut behind him and bowed to the Commandant. Titus was reclining on a sofa, the remains of a meal next to him. The tragedy regarding his daughter had obviously not affected his appetite too much, thought Janus.

'My porter suggests that you have information for me?' said the Commandant. 'I hope this is useful and truthful information. I do intend to carry out the punishment should this matter not be resolved.'

Janus nodded. 'I believe I have discovered the culprit, Sir. I have pieced what little I knew together and followed my instincts. But just to confirm it, does this item look familiar to you?' He held out the necklace and watched the Commandant blanch as he recognised it.

'The cross. Yes. That is my daughter's. Where did you find it?' He reached out his hand and Janus dropped the necklace into his open palm. Titus curled his fingers around it and pressed it against his cheek, closing his eyes. Then he placed it on his lap and rubbed his forehead. He suddenly looked very old.

'I found the cross in the possession of the Prefect Marcus Simplicius Simplex, Sir. He did not report for duty this morning, so, as a friend as well as a colleague, I took it upon myself to visit his quarters.' He dropped his head, as if trying to contain his emotions. 'I found all I needed to know, Sir,' he whispered.

'Tell me!' cried Titus. 'What happened? What did he say?'

Janus shook his head.'He did not speak, Sir. When I found him, he was dead. I believe it was suicide. I found this in his quarters as well.' He handed over a wax tablet. The words ego sum rumex were scratched onto it. I am sorry.

Titus turned the tablet over in his hands.'Where did he get this from?'

Janus shrugged.'I do not know, Sir. I can only suggest that he was improperly pursuing your daughter and she rejected his advances. Our men often saw them together. Why, I was with him myself on several occasions, when he saw you daughter and broke away from me to speak to her.' He frowned. 'She did not look happy with him, Sir. She always seemed to be trying to get away from him; yet he continued to harass the girl. It makes sense, Sir. He was hot tempered. He did not like rejection. I wonder, Sir, whether his passions overruled him one final time.'

Titus stared at the wax tablet, not speaking.'And where is the body now?' he asked finally. 'I take it you did not disturb the scene?'

'No, Sir. As soon as I found him, I came straight over to tell you. I have not mentioned this to any of the men, just in case you required further clarification. I can take you there, Sir, if you want to see for yourself?' Janus offered.

'Yes. Yes, please. I think I need to see this for myself,' he said, suddenly no longer a Commandant but a bereaved father, wanting to see justice done for his daughter.

'As you wish, Sir,' said Janus. Titus stood up and called for a slave. The man Syrus came in and waited for his orders.

'Find my wife. Tell her I believe that we have resolved the situation. I am going to see the remains of the heathen who did this. Then we shall send the message out that the other men are safe. There will be no decimation. Send two of my guards to me and we shall take our leave. Syrus bowed and slipped out of the room. Within moments, two burly guards entered the room and stood to attention.

'Come,' ordered Titus. He turned to Janus and gestured to him to lead the way. 'Take me to this Prefect's quarters.'

Janus led the way across the fort to the barracks. He looked neither right nor left. He was aware that the men he passed were all staring at him and whispering as he went by. Soon the story would be out. Or rather, his version of the story would be out. He would act the concerned friend, of course; tell them in the taverns that he would never have believed it of his friend. Make an offering to Coventina and the water nymphs to aid his friend's redemption in the afterlife. Then, after a while, recruit a new Corax. But he would choose the man more carefully next time.

Janus pushed the door open to Marcus' quarters, and stood back to allow the Commandant access. Titus walked into the room where the bed was. Marcus lay on a blood-soaked straw mattress, a bone-handled knife by his hand. It was clear that the man's throat had been cut. Titus walked towards the bed and stood over the body, staring at it in disgust.

'This man is responsible for my daughter's death,' he said. He stared closely at the body and twisted the head around to see the slash mark. 'Hmm,' he said. 'It is a clean cut. A clean, straight cut. The man did not hesitate. I might have expected a little uncertainty from him whilst he positioned the knife blade.' He moved away from the bed, but left Marcus's head turned towards the door. The once blue eyes stared unseeingly at Janus; stared accusingly, even. Janus had the grace to drop his own gaze to the floor and turn slightly away from the body.

'Have you seen enough, Sir?' he asked, anxious now for the man to leave the room before he made any more comments. Titus shook his head, moving around the room, fingering items here and there. It was as if he was trying to get a feel for this man, trying to decide what had made him do it.

Titus moved aside a piece of cloth that was hanging against the wall. He jumped backwards and roared.

'An altar!' he cried. 'Look! Hidden away in an alcove. The man is a Pagan. He has an altar to his gods in his quarters.'

'Most men here are Pagans, Sir,' said Janus tightly. Titus held his hand up to stop him talking. Janus pressed his lips together, biting against them so hard he almost drew blood. This was taking a great deal of self-control. He willed himself to remain calm.

'Who is this altar dedicated to?' growled Titus. He looked around for his guards. One of them stepped forward and bowed. 'Inspect it. I refuse to touch anything as evil as this piece of stone,' he cried. The man stepped forward and leant into the alcove where the altar was.

'This altar is dedicated to Mithras, Sir,' he said.

'Mithras?' snapped Titus. 'The god who is causing so many problems and so much conflict with the true religion. That temple down there is dedicated to him, is it not?' This time he looked at Janus. 'Answer me!' he shouted as Janus stared back at him like a sullen child. 'Is that temple dedicated to Mithras or not?' Janus curled his hand around the wood of the door, squeezing it so hard he thought a chunk might splinter off in his hand.

'Yes, Sir. The temple is dedicated to Mithras,' he said. His hand moved slowly towards the hilt of his dagger. The second guard moved closer to Janus and grasped the hilt of his sword, staring at the Prefect. Janus relaxed his muscles and dropped his hand back to his side. Later, he promised himself. I will think of a plan later.

Titus whirled around, glaring at the men in the small room.'Then I decree that all worship of the Pagan gods is banned from this fort. It will be banned from Carrawburgh itself. It will be banned from the vicus. He looked directly at Janus. 'I expressly forbid the worship of your deities, as from now,' he said. He pointed at Marcus' body. 'This is what happens when you worship Pagan gods. The men cannot separate reality from their beliefs. They murder innocents for their beliefs. My daughter was a Christian. She was a child of God. This man did not agree with what she believed in and this is the result. I myself saw the error of my ways years ago, and I converted to Christianity. This,' he waved his hand around the room,' is what happens when people do not believe.'

He pushed his way past the guards and past Janus himself and stood on the pathway outside the barracks.

'Use this murderous Prefect as an example,' he shouted. 'The men will not face decimation. They shall instead be called upon to destroy their temple. They must destroy their Sacred Well and their shrines. Let this be a lesson to them. Make it so!'

'But Sir!' cried Janus. 'You do not know if that was the reason he...'

'The reason does not matter!' yelled the Commandant. Janus flinched, despite himself. 'The outcome was the same. My daughter is dead and the man who killed her worshipped Pagan deities!'

Titus stormed back towards the headquarters, calling out orders to his guards as he went. He would have a meeting of the Cohort. He would give the order to destroy the temple and the shrines. And it must be carried out now. Janus stood in the doorway of Marcus' quarters, seething. He waited until the Commandant was a safe distance away and grasped his dagger. With a savage cry, he plunged the blade into the wood with such force that it snapped. Then he punched the door again and again until his knuckles bled and until, in his imagination, he had beaten the Commandant senseless.

After the Commandant's address, the place erupted into mayhem. Men and horses swarmed across the fort and the hillside like ants, yelling and shouting at the people of the vicus to run indoors as they carved their way through the village, spilling out of the fort gates and breaking away in groups to the three sacred sites of Carrawburgh.

Amongst the general confusion and noise, a voice a lot like Marcus's spoke quietly into Janus' ear. *It is your fault that this is happening. You were named for Chaos.* Janus shook his head. He was going mad. It was his imagination. Then he heard a woman's laugh which went on and on and on... He roared to drone the sounds out, and turned, bringing his gladius down on an altar by Coventina's Well. He could not be party to the destruction of the temple. He could desecrate this Well if he had to, but he refused to work on the temple.

The soldiers around him picked up altars and carvings and hurled them into the well, one after another, directed the whole time by the Commandant's guards. The guards surrounded them on their horses, shouting and brandishing their weapons at anyone who dared to hesitate. The water was churning up and splashing over the side as the heavy stones were swallowed into the sacred spring. The men were soaked to the skin in freezing, muddy bog water, slipping around on the still slushy path by the well. Janus and Lucius picked up a large relief of the goddess between them and heaved it over the side of the well, jumping back as a fresh wave swept over the side, drenching them.

Lucius, shivering and dripping, glared at Janus, blaming him for the desecration around them.

'You will pay for this!' he hissed, looking back towards the Mithraic temple. A squad of men were tearing the timber roof off it, and others were throwing their weight against the walls to break them down. Huge warhorses were being forced to push against the stones to weaken the building, and a pile of artefacts lay in a scattered heap outside the temple. One or two men were carrying altars and statues up to the Well, followed by people who had ripped apart the shrine to the water nymphs. There were guards down at the temple, pointing to the Well, telling the soldiers to take the artefacts up there for destruction. Some men were up to their knees in the stream, pulling items which had rolled down the hill out of the water. Suddenly, there was a huge crash and the temple collapsed in on itself. Two of the men who were carrying altars up to the Well paused for breath and turned to see the resulting devastation.

'There were still some altars in there,' said one of them. 'And two statues by the entrance. And the big relief over the main altar as well; they did not get that out.'

The other man nodded. 'Do you realise that I was on the list to join the cult? It could have been me next for initiation. After the stories I have heard, I am pleased it was never so.'

'You have been spared,' replied the other man. 'I always believed it to be a peaceful religion. It seems that was not the case. It is a shame that a minority have spoiled it for the rest of us.'

They watched a minute more as the horses settled and the soldiers were moved away from the temple, then they turned back to their work. They came past Lucius and flung the altars into the Well, flexing their fingers and watching as the water churned up again.

'The cult was always peaceful in the past,' Lucius said to the men. 'Once a madman became in charge, things changed.' He turned away from the Well and limped back to the side of the path where he sat down, rubbing his leg. Janus stared at him in disgust. Another one for my list, he thought and stormed off to the other side of the Well. He pushed some men out of the way and began to smash up a carved stone slab, taking out his frustration on that.

# 1650

'So, this is our enchantrix?' barked the man on horseback. He dismounted, dropping easily to the ground. The man next to him took the reins of the horse from him and led it away to graze in the field next to the Well.

'I'm sorry? I don't understand,' said Meggie. The snow was falling faster now, but her shivers had less to do with the wintry weather and more to do with the panic that was closing in around her. 'What do you mean?'

The man ignored her. He was swathed in a black robe which flapped around his body in the Northumbrian wind. He carried a staff in his hand. Meggie noticed it was carved with all sorts of strange symbols. For some reason, even though the symbols were Christian in design, the staff terrified her. It had a feeling of evil about it. Meggie's sixth sense told her it had tortured and killed; it was soaked in the blood of many people. She looked at it in horror. The man laughed softly and curled his fingers around it tighter.

'She looks at my staff in distaste. She knows what it can prove. Tell me, what is your name girl?'

Meggie's mouth worked but no words would come out.

'Speak up, girl,' barked the man. He cupped his hand around his ear and leaned closer to her. 'I am listening. If you cannot tell me your identity, you will hinder your chances of freedom. I would hate to think I had the wrong person here. I have been charged with finding a witch. Do you understand?'

'A ...witch?' said Meggie. Her voice was cracked and breathless. 'Then, Sir, I am not the person you seek.'

'Oh, you have a voice. That is good. And why do you dispute the claims?'

'Because I am not a witch, Sir,' she said.

'Not a witch? Then why are you here? This is a pagan place of worship. This place stinks of the dark arts. You, my girl, stink of the dark arts. I think you are lying to me.'

'No, Sir! No! I am not a witch. I work with nature, I work with herbs and the goodness Mother Earth provides. I help people, I ease people's suffering, I...'

'She takes lives!' called someone from the back of the group. The men turned. It was a young man called John. He was a farm labourer; Meggie knew he had always harboured a secret love for Alice. Meggie and Alice had giggled over it, talked about his small offerings of love – a posy of wildflowers left on Alice's doorstep, a fresh apple, polished and plucked from a tree, drawn from his apron and given to Alice as he blustered and blushed an excuse...

'John! You know that's not true!' cried Meggie. 'What happened to Alice was...'

'It was murder!' cried another man.

'No!' shouted Meggie. 'Please, no. It wasn't. It was a mistake...' she stopped short as the words of the Roman soldier came back to her. It was a mistake. There have been too many mistakes. She rammed her fist in her mouth and choked back a sob. 'John. You know that's not true, I beg you.'

Nicholson smiled down at Meggie. 'So. We have a young lady here who denies murder. Can she also deny encouraging a man into her abode and attacking him? Drawing blood from an innocent?'

'She used it in a spell!' yelled another man. Meggie recognised him as Robert, Mary's husband; the stupid, deluded idiot, she thought. Mary was the village whore and he pretended he knew nothing about it.

'No! He attacked me!' she shouted back.

'My wife told me otherwise!' Robert called, enjoying the moment, He was a small, thin man whose arms and legs seemed to belong to a different person.

'Your wife should walk around the village with a straw mattress strapped to her back!' cried

Meggie, all reason deserting her. 'It would save her time!'

'Silence!' boomed Nicholson. 'You are an evil woman. You denigrate the women of the village. You cast spells using the blood of innocents. You cause harm to men, women and livestock...'

'No!' shouted Meggie. 'You're lying! I've never harmed livestock..'

'By that, you have admitted you harm men and women,' roared Nicholson.

'No!' cried Meggie, 'I've never intentionally harmed anyone!'

'But you have harmed people!' pressed Nicholson. 'Admit it, Witch. You have harmed people.'

'I...'

'Admit it!'

'Yes, oh please, yes I have. But I never meant it. I never meant to do it. Alice, my dear, sweet Alice; I'm sorry, I'm so sorry,' sobbed Meggie. She crumpled to the floor and pressed her face into the cold, wet grass. There was a thin layer of snow on it now and her cheek was so cold, it felt as if was burning. 'Coventina, blessed Coventina. Goddess of snow, goddess of this place, please help me. Please help me...' she wept into the sacred ground. An image flitted through her mind of the people who had lived here before, who had worshipped at this Well, who had trod the very grass she was lying on. Had Coventina helped them? Would she find it in her heart to help Meggie?

On the fort at Carrawburgh, another figure appeared. It was a man on horseback, looking down at the drama below him. He would wait a little while, he thought, and see what happened. He shivered, then flinched as the shiver jarred his back. He pulled his velvet coat closer to him and looked at the sky. The snow was in for the day. After this was over, it would be nice to go to a local hostelry for a little mulled wine and company, he thought. But he would wait a while and observe it all from up here.

# AD 391

An unsettled silence descended on the area, the night following the desecration of the shrines and temple. The people in the vicus were subdued, having been forced to give up the shrines to their household gods as well as the soldiers giving up theirs in the barracks. Titus had ordered spot checks on the men, to ensure no relics of Paganism remained in the fort. The delights of Aelia and her sisters, the gambling dens and taverns of the vicus held no pull for the soldiers that evening. The bath house was busy; especially in the hot rooms, where the men tried to thaw themselves out and relax after the physical demands of the day.

Janus kept out of the way. He sensed that the rumour mill was grinding and he would not be particularly welcome in the social areas of the fort that evening. He would let them get it out of their system and talk amongst themselves. He would make amends with them over the next few days. He had not lived a double life all this time without learning a few things. It was amazing what some charm and some half-truths could achieve. He was not unduly concerned. And he would deal with Lucius and the Commandant efficiently when the time came. He just had to wait it out, that was all.

He slipped out of his quarters to go for a walk around the edges of the fort. It would burn off some of his adrenalin and help him think.

Janus wandered around the fort, blowing on his hands, trying to warm them up in the silvery glow of the moon. He found himself behind the stables, where he had met Marcus last night. Had it only been last night? He stood by the bench where they had sat, and stared at it. He had done a surprisingly good job of cleaning it up. He had covered the ground with straw afterwards. It had soaked up the worst of the blood, and he burnt it in the furnace to get rid of it. A new covering of straw and a fresh snowfall had covered everything else. He sat down on the bench for a moment, watching a couple of men walk by. He sat very still so they did not see him in the shadows, then he leaned his head back against the wall of the building and closed his eyes. It had been a long, difficult day.

The man Syrus moved quickly and silently. He was a slave; he was unobtrusive. Nobody noticed him. But what they did not realise, was that he was a trained killer himself. His men had been defeated by Titus Perpetuus' troops several years ago. He had been taken prisoner and designated a slave. He could have prevented what had happened to Aemelia, had Titus only listened to him. Instead, he assigned him to other duties and gave Aemelia a female slave the day before it happened. Syrus had tried to explain to his master about the young Prefect who sought his daughter out, but Titus waved him away; other business was more pressing. Syrus had known the fair young man was no danger. He could see genuine affection between the two of them. It was the dark man he did not trust.

He did not know exactly what had happened; Titus had reclaimed Syrus for some other purpose, not even realising his daughter and her new slave were missing. But later that night, he had seen the dark man enter the temple; heard the noises from within, and watched the procession of stunned men leave the temple afterwards, muttering in horror about what they had just witnessed. Syrus had not yet found Olivia. He did not think that he ever would. But he was an intelligent man and knew that, whatever secrets the temple held the dark man was the keeper of them; and Syrus cursed his master for neglecting to listen to him.

And now the dark man was sitting on the bench where he had murdered his friend. Syrus had seen that as well, hidden in the shadows; unobtrusive and unnoticed. Silently, the slave flicked a blade from out of his clothing and moved towards the man on the bench.

In a moment, it was done. The dark man's body slumped to the ground and lay in a pool of blood until the next morning, when the early watch found him. More rumours spread throughout Carrawburgh, with some version of the truth amongst them all. But nobody ever knew for sure what had happened or who had killed Janus. Some said it was the Commandant. Some said it was another member of the cult. Some even said it was the shade of Marcus, come back for his revenge. Nothing was ever proven.

But the temple, the Sacred Well and the shrine to the water nymphs would never be restored. They would fall into disrepair, swallowed up and reclaimed by the earth. The Roman Empire collapsed and the soldiers were moved away from Britannia. What was left of the shrines and their secrets would be discovered again one day. But not for centuries.

# 1650

It happened so fast, that at first she was unaware of it. Whilst Meggie lay sobbing on the snow-covered grass a group of men appeared by her side and roughly hauled her to her feet. They pulled her shawl off her, and yanked her hands around to the front of her body. They bound her wrists with thick, scratchy rope. The rope dug into her skin, ugly, red weals appearing where it bit into her. They dragged her towards Nicholson who looked down on her with contempt.

'She is a suspected charmer, enchantrix and witch,' he intoned. 'We grant this woman fair trial by pricking. If she bleeds, she is not guilty of the aforesaid crimes. If she does not bleed, she shall be dealt with as befits a servant of the Devil. We shall take her to the old temple and try her there. The weather puts in, my friends. The snow is falling thickly and we must take shelter.' He indicated the ruined temple of Mithras that lay between the fort and the Well. It was derelict, but still afforded some shelter. Nicholson did not like feeling damp, or cold, or uncomfortable. The old temple was a heathen place, but he could be persuaded to use it. The sooner this trial was over the better. Meggie was a young, flighty thing. She had shown spirit when she had confronted that man at the back of the group, but he did not like her. She knew too much; he could feel it. The sooner she was tried, the better. Yet he could still be persuaded to change his mind. He liked to see the women beg. He thought lasciviously of the rumours he had heard about this John Kincaid he had been charged with bringing back from Scotland. One woman had been tried twice; the first time, Lieutenant-Colonel Hobson had decided she was too pretty to be a witch and asked for a re-trial. The second time Witchfinder Kincaid had pricked her, the blood had gushed from her thigh and rendered her innocent. It was not beyond the realms of possibility that this blonde creature presently tied up behind him would be acquitted in a similar way.

The company of men half-dragged, half-pulled Meggie to the Mithraic temple. She stumbled several times on the way, her bare feet freezing as she ploughed through frozen mud and her white shift falling off her thin shoulders. All the while, she begged and screamed and cried. She prayed to Coventina, she prayed to Mithras, she begged the water nymphs to take pity on her and help her. The men barged in through the door; but they did not see the man in the shadows peel away from the altar and melt into the wall. They were too intent on demonizing a nineteen year old girl.

'Bring the accused before me!' shouted Nicholson. He had taken up position at the front of the temple, beneath a huge carving of the god slaying a bull. The temple made him feel uncomfortable, but he was determined to do this right now. The thought of the three pounds he could potentially earn drove the uncomfortable feelings out of his mind.

The men who had been dragging Meggie towards the temple threw her down in front of Nicholson. She lay shivering on the stone floor, curled up in a foetal position muttering to herself, repeating Coventina's name and squeezing her eyes shut.

'Make her stand!' growled Nicholson. Two men appeared from the side and forced her to stand upright. Meggie clasped her fingers together, crying and begging for someone to listen to her, for someone to hear what she had to say.

'Take her clothes off. Strip her to the waist!' said Nicholson. The men looked at one another. Who was going to do this?

'Strip her!' shouted Nicholson. 'What keeps you? For God's sake, if you won't do that, then lift her clothing and pull it over her head. I must have her lower body exposed. That is where the blood will settle if she is human. I need to prick her to test her. Do you want this witch vanquished? Do you want her out of your village? Then do it! Strip her! Now!'

John stepped forward. His face was grey and his eyes huge and terrified.'I shall do it, Sir. I feel I owe it to Alice to have her convicted. She killed my Alice and she must pay.'

John!' cried Meggie, some of her senses returning to her. 'Please, no. What would Alice think? How can this help her?'

'You killed her,' he spat out. 'You killed her and you need to pay.'

With that, he lunged forward and grabbed hold of the hem of Meggie's shift. He yanked it over her head and tried to ignore the muffled screams and cries of shame and humiliation. Nicholson's eyes glinted as he scanned the girl's body. It was milk-white and slender, her breasts small and her stomach flat. Perfect. She was a joy to behold. He would make this last.

'What is this witch's name? It is correct practice that someone confirms the identity of the accused. I shall not be held responsible for harming an innocent,' said Nicholson, looking around at the assembled men in the temple.

'Meggie. It is definitely Meggie,' cried John, stepping forward. There was a stifled cry from the girl who stood half naked in front of the men she had grown up with.

'Yes. It is Meggie,' said Robert. 'Make the witch suffer.' There was a rumble of assent from the men and Meggie moaned softly. She was struggling to breathe, her face trapped inside the material of her shift. She shook her head to try and slacken it off, but it wrapped itself tighter and she began to choke and cough. She raised her hands to her face to try and pull the cloth away, but somebody grabbed her hands and pulled them down. She twisted her hands, trying to loosen the rope which bound her wrists, but the fibres bit in even more. She gagged and coughed again. Nicholson wrinkled his nose and viewed her with contempt.

'It is the demon inside her trying to escape,' said Nicholson. He raised his staff and showed the men the wicked pin on the end of it. 'I shall prick the witch with this tool. I shall need to find a witch-mark first. I shall approach the accused and look at her body.' Nicholson stepped towards Meggie and inspected every inch of the flesh that was exposed. He was so close she could feel his hot breath on her body. His breathing was ragged and she wanted to pull away from him, but she was held fast by his men. His voice spoke next to her ear, his face invisible to her. 'Do not struggle, Witch. If you are innocent, you have nothing to fear.' Meggie could feel the icy cold seeping through the broken stone slabs on the floor, numbing her feet and creeping up her legs. She thought she would faint with cold and humiliation. Then she prayed that she would lose consciousness; it would make this more bearable if she was oblivious to it.

# 2010

Liv turned her back on Ryan. Honestly, he was being completely annoying today. She'd sometimes had the impression that he wanted to become a bit more than a friend. She'd known him since primary school; they'd grown up together like brother and sister, been best friends for years. She'd always dismissed him as anything else. But lately he'd started to look at her in a strange way. He'd draw his eyebrows together and stare at her when he thought she couldn't see him. And she could tell he was thinking stuff that hadn't entered his mind before. She'd given it some thought herself, to be honest. She was going to say something or at least let him know he had a chance with her if he'd behaved himself today. But that was out of the question now. He was driving her mad. She felt an unreasonable, simmering anger bubble up inside her and quashed it firmly. She knew he hated stuff like this. His thing was sport and geography and science; nothing 'girly' like history, as he kept telling her.

'Liv?' Ryan tried again. 'I'm sorry, Liv. But honestly. I did see someone next to you. He held his hand up a few inches above Liv's head. 'Here. He was about up to here and he was standing right beside you.'

Liv sighed.

'Look, Ryan,' she said quietly. 'I know you don't really want to be here with me. It's fine. You go on home. The bus will be coming past again shortly. I can finish up here, and write my notes when it's nice and quiet. Then I'll see you tomorrow.'

'Liv...'

'No. Please. Just... go home,' she said. She turned back to the altars and squatted down again. She couldn't let the idea of Marcus slip away from her. She needed to understand how they worshipped here and how they lived here. She was desperate to absorb the atmosphere and try to feel something of the place. She closed her eyes and breathed deeply, letting her surroundings fade away. Liv gasped as an image, not of a Roman soldier, came to her; but of a young girl standing in the temple with fair hair. The young girl was holding her hand out and Liv opened her eyes quickly, looking around her.

'What on earth...?' she said. She turned to see if Ryan was still around, automatically wanting to mention it to him but he'd disappeared. Of course he had. She'd told him in no uncertain terms to go, hadn't she? Liv sighed. It was too complicated to think about. She stood up and shuffled her papers together. Maybe she should go and write up her notes. She shivered and looked at the sky. It was a cloudless blue, but there was a distinct chill in the air. She turned away from the altars and walked back towards the entrance. She paused at the place where the door would have been. There was a whispering noise behind her, like a chanting or something. It got louder and louder. Then she heard a scream. Liv jumped and turned back to face the altars. A bird of prey was curving away from the temple. It must have been that. But she had the definite impression that she had just missed something. Something had happened when she had turned her back. She looked around her again, wishing Ryan hadn't actually listened to her and left her on her own. Too late now, she thought. She hurried out of the temple, and found a patch of grass to sit down on, throwing her backpack on the ground next to her.

Liv spread her papers around her, weighing them down with heavy stones from the field. She pulled a pen and a notebook from her backpack and chewed the end of the pen as she decided what to write. Her mind wandered as she stared at the blank sheet of paper before her, and she thought again of the strange chanting.

Then a girl's voice broke into her thoughts. *Blessed Coventina, save me.*

Liv froze, her pen out of her mouth and halfway to the notebook. An eerie silence

descended over the countryside and Liv felt
something flutter down from the sky and touch her
skin like a butterfly kiss. Then she felt another. And
another. She looked up and saw a cloud rolling in
across the field, bringing with it a blizzard. The
snowflakes fell faster and faster, and Liv scrambled
to her feet, stuffing everything into her backpack.

'Typical!' she cried, looking around for
some sort of shelter. Her best bet was the bushes
and trees up near the fort. This weather hadn't been
forecast, she was sure. She lifted her bag and
balanced it on her head as she ran, cursing Ryan for
taking the waterproofs and umbrella with him. She
had made him put them in his backpack – her
excuse was that her bag was full of notes for her
project. And she didn't think that she would have
fallen out with Ryan like that. They'd had squabbles
in the past, but he'd never annoyed her to that
extent; or indeed walked off and left her when she'd
ordered him away in the past. She ducked her head
and hurtled through the field. Then she wasn't sure
what happened, but one minute she stumbled and
righted herself, pelting onwards, and in the next
minute, she was in the entrance to the temple,
looking at a tableaux of such horrific proportions
that all she could do was stare in horror and open
her mouth and scream.

# 1650

Nicholson circled Meggie three times. He pressed his grimy, rough fingertips all over her body, squeezing and nipping her, kneading her flesh, trying to find a witch-mark. He wanted a beauty spot, or a small mole. Anything he could see that would justify the trial.

'There!' his voice was strong and excited. 'She bears the mark of the Devil. A brown circle beneath her breast. Look, men, see the filthy witch's mark?' He pointed at a perfectly round mole, dark against the white skin where Meggie's breast met her torso. The men crowded around her and murmured their assent.

'It is. I see the witch's mark,' said Robert. He reached out and poked it for himself. Meggie flinched and spat out a curse. These men were evil. They were filthy. She had never in her life cursed anyone before; but this was a situation she had never dreamed she would be in. They thought she was a witch, a servant of the Devil; evil incarnate. She felt dirty and abused, pawed all over by these wicked men, trying to prove something that was untrue. She felt the ground sway beneath her and again prayed that blessed oblivion might carry her away.

'Behold, gentlemen. I shall prick the fiend and test her,' cried Nicholson. He raised the staff and again displayed the evil point on the end of it. He made sure nobody ever touched this staff. Its secret was too precious. For hidden in the shaft, was a small mechanism which was under his control. The sharp point, which now glinted in the frosty light from the temple entrance, was retractable. Cuthbert Nicholson had only to tweak a small lever worked into the carvings on the staff and the point disappeared. This left only a blunt end of wood which he would press against a woman's thigh. By this method, he had control over who he tortured and who survived. He was a fickle man. If he needed money, he would find a witch or two easily. If his purse hung heavy and full by his side, he was more lenient. But he was a greedy man; and the leniency was becoming less and less evident.

Nicholson's eyes flickered over Meggie again, but decided this one was different. He wanted to see the fear in her eyes as he pressed the staff against her thigh. He wanted to see her thin little face crumple and her lips tremble as he carried out the test.

'Men, I am about to test the witch. You Sir,' he nodded at John. 'Reveal the witch's face to me. Her body must be tested, but her face must be visible. I must see whether she moves her lips in a chant or a spell to produce the blood which might prove her to be human.'

John ripped the dress down from Meggie's face. He held the fabric away from her, so her body was revealed and her face was free. Meggie gasped for air and opened her eyes. She was looking straight at Nicholson; to his great delight he saw her confusion turn into fear as she registered the point he held up to her eye level. This would be a joy. He curled the edges of his mouth into a sneer and held her gaze.

Mesmerised by his eyes and frozen by terror, Meggie did not see the swift move as he stabbed the staff into her thigh. She felt the cold wooden edge pushing against her skin. Her eyes opened wide and her mouth formed a silent 'o' as she realised she could not feel the pin stabbing her. She looked down, seeing no blood running out of her body.

'She is a witch!' screeched Nicholson. 'She does not bleed. Look! She has failed the pricking. She bears a witch mark. We have heard foul curses stream out of her mouth in this pagan temple. I declare this woman to be a witch; a child of the Devil. Take her away! Deal with her as appropriate!'

'No!' cried Meggie as the men seized her and began to drag her away. 'No! Please, do the test again. I beg you; I'm not a witch. Please. It's the cold weather – it makes the blood stay within my body. It has settled within me. I am not a witch…'

'Very well!' cried Nicholson. 'I shall test you again.' He raised the staff and prepared to prick Meggie once more. Then there was a blood-curdling scream from the entrance to the temple. Nicholson looked up and his face filled with horror. The staff wavered in the air, as if he was unsure of what to do with it. Meggie managed to turn around; she saw the men who were by the door fall to their knees as a black shape sped through the middle of the temple.

'Blessed Coventina!' cried Meggie. 'You came to save me! Merciful goddess, prove to these men I am not a witch!' She knelt and raised her bound hands to the shadow, imploring it for help. It was the shape of a slender, young woman. She had long, dark hair and her clothes clung to the outline of her body. The image was hazy, but as it approached Meggie, it leaned towards her, reaching out its hand. Meggie had seen spirits and shades before, but nothing like this. It had to be Coventina, it had to be.

'Demon!' cried Nicholson. 'The witch has summoned a demon. Get thee back to Hell!' he shouted. He raised the staff in the air and grasped it with both hands. He brought it down with a crack across Meggie's shoulders. The girl let out a cry and crumpled onto the stone floor, falling face forwards.

Nicholson raised his staff again and this time thrust it point first into Meggie's back. He stabbed again and again, repeating his accusations, until even his men were sickened by what they saw. Three of the men wrestled Nicholson's weapon away from him. The girl was obviously dead; she lay unnaturally twisted on the ground, blood congealing around her, matting her hair and soaking her clothing. Someone had the decency to throw a cloak over her and they led Nicholson to the side of the temple. He was still hurling abuse at Meggie, even whilst they tried to reason with him.

John staggered outside and vomited. Robert crawled out shortly afterwards and sat beside him, his face pale. The images of what he had just witnessed replayed over and over in his mind's eye. John wiped his mouth and turned to speak to the older man.

'She bled,' he whispered. 'She wasn't a witch.'

Robert shook his head.'No. But she's something queer. She summoned up something in there. What else could that…thing…be?'

'I thought it was maybe Alice,' choked out John. His eyes filled with tears and they spilled down his cheeks. He looked helplessly at Robert. 'Maybe Alice. Coming to help her.' Robert shrugged.

'I don't know. She would have called her by name, surely, if it was Alice,' he said.

John dropped his head into his hands. 'What's going to happen to her? They can't leave her here like that, can they?' he whispered.

There was a commotion from the temple, and Nicholson stormed out. He was no longer restrained by his lackeys, but they guarded him closely as he left; Robert thought it was for his own protection.

'Remove it from the temple. Take it away and burn it. Reduce it to ash and scatter the ashes in running water,' rambled Nicholson. 'The place where we found the witch- it was a spring. It was the source of this stream that runs past us. Take the body there and burn it... Tell nobody what we witnessed here. Let it be known that she was a witch. Let anyone who defies my findings be condemned as a witch or a wizard. They shall meet the same fate without the trial. Only a person who harbours a dark side would have seen anything in there; anything that happened in there. Do you understand? Do you understand?' He leant down and screamed the last three words in John's ear. John flinched and nodded. Nicholson fixed Robert with the same gimlet stare and waited for a response. Robert stared at him and inclined his head. Satisfied, Nicholson stormed off and ordered someone to clear the temple.

One of the men, who had been sent to escort Nicholson - perhaps Bell- left the temple with a bloodied bundle slung over his shoulder. John retched again and Robert looked the other way, across the field to the ruined fort. He saw a man up there on horseback. Charles Hay. He was watching to see what the outcome was. Hay didn't have to wait long before the smoke began to curl upwards into the slate-grey sky. It had stopped snowing now, but the landscape was blanketed in white and the clouds were hanging heavy with the promise of a fresh fall before evening.

Long before the new snow came, the pyre had burnt out and the so-called witch's ashes had been scattered in the burn which sprang from Coventina's Well. The water swept the ashes away and tossed them downstream, where they danced and whirled, flowing eventually into the River South Tyne. Meggie had always believed Coventina made the ice melt and the winter thaw. And nobody thought to wonder why the Dene Burn hadn't frozen over that day.

Nobody gave the flowing water more than a fleeting thought as they left the Well and straggled back to the village in silence. Nobody, that is, except Charles Hay.

Two days later, Charles brought his horse down the hillside and rode it past the temple. Hay felt no emotion as he followed the track towards

Coventina's Well. He walked the horse slowly past the burn which gurgled as it ran through the field. He pulled the horse up by the Well and gazed into the water. He leaned over to peer into it. Was that where they had thrown the ashes? He had heard tell they'd scattered them somewhere. He thought he could make something out in the depths of the pool. It looked like a person. He frowned. They'd burnt the body, he'd seen it. It must be a trick of the light. Whatever they had done, as far as he was concerned, it was good riddance. The girl had been a menace to society, guilty of attempted murder no less. Why should she have been spared? As he reasoned with himself, a movement behind the stone wall of the Well made him look.

A young woman slipped out of the shadows; dark haired and dark eyed, she stared curiously at Hay. She gazed at him brazenly for a while without speaking.

'What is it?' Charles snapped eventually. 'Why do you stare at me?' She was starting to make him feel more than a little uncomfortable.

The girl blinked and tilted her head to one side.

'Is this yours?' she asked, not answering his question. She held up her hands, offering him something she clasped in her palms. Despite the wintry conditions, the girl stood in a loose, white gown which lifted gently in the wind. She didn't shiver or seem cold in the slightest. Hay glared at her, not trusting her.

'Show me what you have,' he stated. 'I do not come here regularly, so I doubt anything you find would belong to me.'

'I have seen you before,' she said. 'You were on the fort two days ago, watching, were you not?'

Charles felt unsettled by this woman. She spoke evenly and quietly; she did not take her eyes off him for an instant.

'Do you know who I am?' he said. 'I am allowed access wherever I care to go. It is not my problem if I stumble upon something distasteful.'

'It is you who caused the problem, Mr Hay,' said the girl. Charles started. He hadn't mentioned his name to her at all.

'No. It was not me,' he answered. 'It was a misunderstanding between some villagers, that's all.'

'A mistake, Mr Hay?' asked the girl. She held her hands out a little further. 'Please, tell me. Is this yours?'

Hay glared at her. He didn't recognise her at all. She wasn't a village girl; her voice was accented slightly he realised. Was she a traveller? Or a gypsy? He noticed a thin golden ring on her finger and a golden cross around her neck. So she had some things of value, he thought. The ring was intricately carved and no doubt stolen from some poor sap she had fleeced.

'Show me,' he repeated, nodding at her hands. They were white, smooth hands. Not the hands of a worker.

The girl unfurled her hands and presented Charles with the object; a small, sharp bladed knife. Bone-handled and slim, he recognised it from Meggie's house. It was the knife she had used to stab him in her pathetic attempt at self-defence.

'No!' he cried, blanching. 'No, that's not mine. I don't know who it belongs to. I've never seen it before...'

'Haven't you?' whispered the girl. Her eyes flickered away from his face and she fixed her gaze over his shoulder. Charles twisted around in his saddle. On the hillside opposite, he saw a faint, white shape. It seemed to be the outline of a person. As he looked, it began to walk towards him.

'He is here,' whispered the dark haired girl from behind him. 'Come; come to us.' Hay whipped his head around to shout at the girl, but she had vanished.

'What the...?' he cried and twisted around again. The dark haired girl was on the other side of his horse, and the figure in white was standing right behind her. The horse whinnied and pranced. Charles hung on to the reins.

'Charles Hay,' said the figure in white. It stepped out from behind the dark haired girl and raised its hand. Now he could see that the gown was not white – it was stained with blood and ripped in several places as if a blade had thrust into it. 'A curse be upon you; you will pay for your errors of judgement. I curse you with all my powers and all my knowledge. I curse you for the harm you have inflicted on other people and the women you have violated. I curse you for your actions, your thoughts your words and your deeds. Suffer, Charles Hay, as you have made others suffer.'

Nobody was near enough to hear Charles Hay scream or to hear his cries for mercy. Nobody was there to hear him choke his last breath out. They found him soon afterwards, his body floating in the seven feet of water in Coventina's Well. They couldn't explain how his throat had been cut or how he had ended up in the water. They put it down to murder; but there was never a manhunt. Perhaps a vagabond, or a traveller had done it, they said. Some even said he had inflicted the wound himself, out of guilt. They had found a small, bone-handled knife on the edge of the Well; maybe he had dropped it as he had fallen? Nobody would ever know.

And far up on the ruins of Carrawburgh, a hazy figure stood watching the scene below. She had always loved it here, and now she was part of it forever.

# 2010

It was fuzzy and unclear through the blizzard, but what Liv saw could not be doubted. A group of men seemed to be pawing a young, half-naked girl, and the sides of the temple were lined with other men watching. It all happened in silence. One man, a dark, cloaked figure seemed to thrust something into the girl's leg.

Liv began to run through the central aisle, but it was like running through treacle.

'Stop it! Stop it!' she cried. Her legs wouldn't move fast enough, but she gave no thought to what she would do when she actually got to the people. A group of other men seized the girl. The girl twisted around to face Liv, and then dropped to her knees. The image of the girl raised her bound hands to Liv and Liv automatically reached out to her. Then, just as quickly, the shape of the man with the staff hit the girl across the shoulders and she slumped to the ground.

'No!' shouted Liv. She threw herself towards the girl and her hand clasped around nothing. The image disappeared, but the snow still came down, falling thickly, covering the altars and the statues. Liv didn't feel cold, but she was shaking. She stood up and stared at the spot where the girl had been. A name suddenly popped into her head.

'Meggie,' she said out loud, startling herself. 'The witch whose ashes they put in the burn. I think I'm cracking up. It's all that research...' Liv stood for a moment, the girl's face clear in her mind. Then she backed away from the altars, as if she was in a trance. Her bag lay forgotten where she had dropped it and she turned as she reached the old lobby. Liv left the temple, not thinking about where she was going.

It was as if something had taken control of her body. Automatically, she headed towards the kissing gate and followed the path around the edge of the temple.

*I have to go to the Well*, she told herself. *I need to go to Coventina's Well*. She drifted across the little wooden plank that made a bridge across the stream. Her footsteps barely showed in the fresh snowfall. She turned right, and moved towards the Well. Her mind was full of strange words and images. There was the girl at the temple, who had to be fair-haired Meggie. Then another face appeared to her. A dark haired, dark eyed girl who seemed to be waiting by the side of the path. There was a hum of voices, more chanting and then the dark haired girl whipped her head around, her expression changing into one of fear then anger.

*'Vos proditor mihi. Quod iam vos capto dico mihi is eram a erroris.'*

Then Liv heard a man's voice answering her.

*'Is eram. Puto mihi. Ego did non vilis is.'*

*'Vos iuguolo mihi.'*

*'Ego sum rumex. commodo indulgeo mihi. ego diligo vos.'*

*...you betrayed me. And now you tell me it was a mistake*

*...it was. Believe me. I did not mean it.*

*...you killed me*

*...I am sorry. Please forgive me. I love you*

'Stop it!' sobbed Liv. 'I don't know what's going on. I don't want to hear all this!' She covered her ears with her hands and stumbled onwards, trying to squeeze her eyes shut, but the images kept on coming and the voices kept on talking.

Liv found herself standing by the remains of Coventina's Well. She was trembling and crying, rubbing at her eyes with the back of her hand. She stared into the muddy pool, and again all sorts of images flashed through her mind - men throwing altars and statues into the water; a young girl kneeling by the side of it, whispering mystical words and casting handfuls of herbs into it. A man floating face down in it, his white shirt ballooning up around his lifeless body...

KIRSTY FERRY

Liv felt something hard and cold being pressed into her hand and she gasped as she looked down and saw a tiny, bone-handled knife clutched in her fingers.

'Oh no, please. This isn't right!' she cried. She turned around, looking for whoever had pushed it into her palm; a shimmering, glowing figure melted into the hillside and a dark shape formed on the top of the fort.

*Servo vestri*, urged a girl's voice. *Protect yourself. You cannot trust him. Learn by our mistakes...*

'Who is this?' cried Liv. 'Where are you?'

*We are everywhere*, whispered the voice. *We are the Guardians of this place...*

As Liv stared at the spot where she thought the voice was coming from, she felt a light pressure on her shoulder. A hand grasped it and then sharply pulled her around to face its owner.

# 2010

A man's face swam in front of Liv's. All she could see clearly were his blue eyes pleading with her. She tried to pull away from him, a scream catching in her throat.

'Please tell her,' begged the man. 'Tell Aemelia I am sorry. It was a mistake...'

'You killed me!' cried a girl. It was the dark-haired one; the one whose face had flashed in front of Liv's vision. 'I cannot forgive you for that.' Liv somehow understood the words. She felt the crushing pain of both the man and the woman physically draining her. She tried to shake the man's hand off her shoulder, but he held her in a strong grip; an unearthly cold was burning through her clothing and touching her skin.

'They made me, I had no choice. I did not know!' said the man.

'He's telling the truth,' said a female voice. 'Aemelia, allow him a chance to explain. You know his action was pre-destined. It's all a part of what we are...' The blonde girl from the temple appeared out of the blizzard. Her white shift gleamed like frost against the snow.

'No,' replied the dark girl sharply. 'It is too late. He has no place here and I have work to do.

Meggie, ask him to leave. I want no part of his dishonesty.'

Liv flinched as the man's hand gripped her shoulder even tighter. The atmosphere was oppressive, the snow still whirling around. Liv began to sob. She didn't understand any of this. The man's grip slackened on her shoulder and he turned to face the dark eyed girl: Aemelia. Aemelia's shape blurred into the snow and disappeared and the man followed a fraction of a second afterwards.

The fair haired girl watched them vanish and her shoulders slumped as if in defeat. Then she turned to face Liv. The spirit girl moved closer to Liv, watching her intently. It was as if she was trying to work something out, as if she recognised her on some level. Liv had the sudden urge to apologise to her, to say she was sorry for not saving her from the man with the stick and the mob in the temple. Without thinking, Liv reached out to her. Meggie reached out at the same time, and had there been any substance to Meggie's form, their fingers would have touched. Liv forced herself to stay still, although her knees were threatening to buckle under her at any minute. She managed to stay upright and her breath came in frightened little bursts as Meggie stared at her unblinkingly. It seemed to Liv that Meggie had become a little clearer, more solid looking. Yet she knew in her heart what this girl was.

'You were there at the temple,' Meggie said eventually. Her voice was clear and soft, rolling with a Northumbrian burr that Liv had never considered. 'I know who you are now. I thought you were Coventina. I thought you had come to save me.' Her face twisted a little, the painful memory returning. 'I understand why nobody came. I've learnt the reasons.' Liv opened her mouth to protest but Meggie tilted her head to one side and smiled. 'No, don't worry,' she continued. 'This is a strange place. Sometimes our worlds collide. You and I were there at different times, but our spirits are connected. It's like Aemelia. She couldn't stop what happened to me; but she had gone before, and she wanted to protect me in the only way she could. Aemelia doesn't have my beliefs. She learned to accept them when she became a Guardian here. If only she would accept his.' She shook her head. 'Perhaps now you are here, we can close the circle and she can listen to him. Truly listen to him, with her heart as well as her mind. She knows she is part of this, as much as I am.'

'I –I wish I could have saved you,' whispered Liv. 'If I'd only been there properly...' Meggie smiled slightly, a vestige of bitterness in it. Yet Liv knew she wasn't blaming her.

'You couldn't have saved me, even if you had been at my side as a sister,' said Meggie. 'Nobody could have. I accept that now. The same thing would have happened to you. You see things like I did. You feel things. That is why the spirits have brought you here. I would have feared for you. He would have taken you as well.'

'Who would have taken me? The man who...the man who..' she couldn't bring herself to say 'killed you'.

'Yes. Him. But you would have faced a worse demon before that.' Meggie frowned, remembering. 'All I wanted was to be peaceful and to be loved. I only wanted to help people. But it went wrong...all because of Charles Hay. I can't forgive him for what he did to me. And for what he did to Alice.' Meggie moved closer to Liv and laid her translucent hands over Liv's. A current of energy flowed into her and Liv cried out as a succession of images flashed through her mind like a film reel. There was a young girl with laughing eyes, then the same girl lying dead in a filthy cottage. An image of a church and then the sensation of being manhandled out of the building. There was crying and begging and finally a man's face with arrogant eyes staring at her accusingly.

'What did you do?' asked Liv. 'What did I just see?'

'I showed you some of my life,' said Meggie, satisfied. 'I was right. We do have a connection. You wouldn't have seen it otherwise.

Charles Hay. He is the one who is to blame. My poor Alice. She was only seventeen. '

'I'm seventeen,' whispered Liv. 'And that girl. Was it Alice? She looked like me.'

'She's a lot like you, isn't she?' said Meggie. 'She had dark hair like yours. And the same colour eyes.' Meggie raised one hand and stroked Liv's hair. It felt to Liv as if a gentle breeze were lifting the dark strands. Meggie smiled sadly. 'Hay would have taken you as he took her. But Alice is safe now. He lost the power to hurt her when she died. It was the people she left behind who felt the pain. It was me who killed Alice. It was my fault. I should never have given her the potion. I would never have hurt her willingly, though. Do you understand that?' Meggie stared at Liv, as if asking for absolution from this girl who looked so much like her friend.

'Those people were cruel!' said Liv. 'They were all evil. You weren't a witch at all. I'm so sorry...' she began to cry, feeling ridiculous that Meggie's words could have affected her like this. She remembered the story of the witch's ashes flowing through the burn and felt helpless.

'They just didn't know any better,' said Meggie. 'But Alice didn't blame me.' Meggie laughed, disbelievingly. 'She told me afterwards, you know. She managed to come back and find me. I shouldn't have been surprised. This place is full of

221

something magical. So much has happened here, but it can affect people in different ways, you know. I used to see the soldier on the fort up there. You saw him too, didn't you?'

A memory flashed into Liv's mind from earlier that morning – the dark shape up on Carrawburgh. It seemed an age ago.

'That was a soldier?' whispered Liv. She blanched, suddenly realising something 'Was he the one who was talking about Aemelia?' She looked around her, trying to see a vestige of the couple who had been speaking in the strange language. Latin. It had been Latin.

'I hope they can finally make peace,' sighed Meggie. 'This sacred place of ours – we guard it and protect it, but there has always been something missing. I think that's what you're here for. You were drawn to it, weren't you? Just like we were. Knowledge and passion are so very powerful. I...' Suddenly, she looked up, and stared behind Liv's head. Meggie's eyes widened and a look Liv could not identify flashed across her face. It was fear and horror and shock, all mixed together.

'No! No! What is he doing here?'

Meggie still had hold of one of Liv's hands, and Liv felt her clutch it tighter. It was an instinctive reaction – even now, whoever this person was, he could affect her like this.

Liv turned quickly. The man she had glimpsed in her vision was staring at Meggie with the same arrogant eyes he had possessed in life. This man's spirit was dark; almost as dark as the soldier's and Liv knew it was Charles Hay. His spirit was made of a blackness that was different to that of the soldier. The soldier had radiated sorrow, self-hatred and regret. This man emanated pure evil. Liv shrank away as the man moved silently, a dark shadow leaching into the area around the Well.

'Praise be to the forces that have released me,' he said quietly. 'Yet look at this place. It is nothing more than a piece of boggy ground. It has no power over anybody now. I have waited a long time for this.' He approached Meggie and Liv. Liv felt Meggie's hand contract even more around her fingers.

'You can't harm us any more,' whispered Meggie. 'Our power is greater than your evil. As Guardians of Coventina's Well and servants of the sacred deities that protect this place, we order you to leave.' Liv could feel a slight tremor in Meggie's hand. The shimmering figure wavered as if the ghost of Hay was draining her energy somehow.

'Whose power?' sneered Hay. 'You have no power. You are the same as you were – a sad, lonely witch who wanders the moors because nobody wants you. Oh, poor, dear, little Meg.' In one swift motion, he left the place where he stood and was at Meggie's side. Meggie's shape flickered again. Liv could tell she was losing confidence. The man who had haunted her life was still haunting her death.

Liv looked around, searching for Aemelia. She knew Meggie needed Aemelia's strength and sent a silent plea out to the universe for Aemelia to return. The Guardians had to work together to protect the area from evil and treachery. Meggie and Aemelia had turned it back into a sacred place and wiped the brutality away from it. They had cleansed it. Hay couldn't be allowed to tarnish it any more. Liv saw two figures on the fort, faint through the still-falling snow: Aemelia and her soldier.

'She's on the fort!' burst out Liv. 'They're both up there...'

Hay whipped his head around and those arrogant eyes were staring at Liv. 'What is she?' he asked, his voice full of scorn. 'Does she protect this place as well?' He pushed his face right up to Liv's and Liv felt sickened. His hair was hanging around his face, some of it still tied back in a ragged old ribbon, and his shirt was dripping what might have been water all over the ground. A jagged cut ran from one side of his neck to the other. Another current of energy flowed through Meggie's hand and once again Liv saw flashes of what had happened. This man was cursed; she gagged as she visualised his death. It was almost as bad as Meggie's; but worse in that fact that nobody wielded the knife that killed him. She saw him clutch his neck and fall from his horse, coughing and choking as the blade cut deep into the flesh. Blood spurted out of his veins and he writhed on the ground trying to fend off his invisible attacker. At the end of it, a white mist wrapped itself around his body. It lifted him up and the body was tossed into the Well, as if it was completely weightless.

'Ah. Another enchantrix, yes? Another charmer. You are part of this then. I see my Meg has taught you well,' hissed Hay, reading the terror in Liv's eyes. 'Can you see what happened to me? What she did to me? Do not be fooled by her. She is a murderess. Did she tell you she killed her best friend? Poor, little Alice. So sad. Yet, you look so like her. I could almost…' He reached his hand out and touched her hair as Meggie had done. Only this time, it was like cold, slimy seaweed wrapping around her skull and she ducked away from him.

'Be strong, Olivia,' murmured Meggie, staring at Hay in disgust. 'He can't hurt you…'

There was a humming noise in Liv's ears and the atmosphere shifted. She staggered a little as Aemelia appeared by the trio. Aemelia grasped Meggie's free hand, and held her own up. Some inexplicable force flung Hay away from Liv. He growled and tried to push back through them, into the centre of the odd little circle, but something was stopping him.

'Olivia,' Aemelia said. She spoke in heavily accented English now. 'I know that name.' Her sloe-black eyes cleared as she remembered something else. 'She took me to him. She was paid well for it. But he killed her anyway. Then he took the money back.'

'It's not her,' said Meggie. 'Let it go. Marcus has come to you asking for forgiveness…'

'Marcus?' asked Liv. 'So that's his altar..?'

'What?' snarled Aemelia, turning on Liv. 'That man tells me stories he expects me to believe, then you tell me that you know about the altar. That temple is an insult to Christianity.'

'No!' cried Liv. 'It wasn't like that!'

'Silence!' ordered Aemelia. 'You know nothing.'

'Aemelia,' said Meggie, a warning in her voice. She was stronger now that Hay was contained. 'It is thanks to this girl that Marcus has found you. She was meant to come here, as we were, to help us; and you have accepted my beliefs, so why can't you do the same with Marcus? You did before. He hasn't changed. He's been trapped here alone. We at least had each other. Take her hand. If we can somehow close the circle, we can stop this. We can send...him...back and we can help Marcus...'

Aemelia stared at Liv and dropped her hand slightly. She frowned, looking through Liv at something only she could see. Finally satisfied, she raised her chin and touched her fingertips tentatively to Liv's arm. She did not feel ready to touch her hand just yet, but she spoke softly.

'My Olivia betrayed me. She led me straight into that other man's trap. I cannot move away from that. Your name... it holds many memories for me.' The thought confused her. It took enough away from her concentration to break whatever control she had over Hay. He took his chance, feeling the release as his bindings broke. With a great roar he reared up.

'You are all witches!' he screamed. Meggie cried out, and sent one more burst of energy towards Liv. It flickered and fizzed between their fingertips. The energy flashed around the girls, encircling them like a haze of fireflies, but not before Hay managed to burst through the centre of the group, a black ball of energy breaking them up. The girls were forced apart and Liv felt a burning in her palm where she still held the small bone-handled knife.

Then it was as if something possessed her. She knew what she had to do. She raised her arm and shouted as she drove the blade into the black mass that was Hay. The black mass fractured apart with a horrible hissing sound and an animal-like howl rent the air. Liv felt herself being lifted off her feet by the force and the world splintered about her. She tumbled backwards towards the Well; but instead of landing in the shallow, boggy water, she gasped as a curtain of ice closed over her head and she fell down and down, the water filling her nose and her mouth, rushing into her ears and drowning out all of her senses.

# 2010

'Liv! Liv!'

The voice seemed to come from very far away. Liv could feel herself being shunted around, bobbing about like a cork in the ocean. She wasn't cold. She hadn't felt cold the whole time she'd been in the snowstorm. Odd that. But she was wet. She was wet now and her head was hurting and all she could see was a procession of images and figures imprinted on her minds' eye. Images of Meggie and Aemelia, and Marcus and Charles Hay. Images of the Mithraic temple and Coventina's Well. Emotions pressed into her consciousness. Betrayal. Loss. And lies. Huge lies. Why did everybody lie?

'Liv. Get up.' Then some swearing. 'Can I not just leave you for ten sodding minutes without you doing something stupid?'

More shaking. And more wetness. Liv began to cough and splutter as she choked on something. She felt a hand grasping her shoulder and her eyes flew open. Ryan. Ryan with half a bottle of water in his hand. Evidently, she was wearing the other half. Hence the wetness.

'What's going on?' asked Ryan. 'I leave you in the temple, and I find you out here.' He gestured around him, more droplets of water splashing about.

Liv was sprawled flat on her back in the field near the Well. Her belongings were scattered around her, the lace on her boots untied. She sat up painfully. She ached in places she didn't know she could ache. Her head was pounding and her mouth was dry. The only bit of her above the neck that was dry, she thought ironically. He must have been pouring it onto her to wake her up. She indicated that she wanted the water, and snatched it from him as he offered it to her. She took a huge swig from the bottle, staring around her, blinking in the afternoon sunlight until she felt she could speak again without croaking

'Where's the snow?' Liv asked eventually. 'Where's it all gone?'

'What?' asked Ryan. 'What snow? It's been hot and sunny all afternoon. I've been having a wander up there.' He nodded towards the car park. 'I had a cuppa, and walked along the Wall a bit, while I was waiting for you.' He shrugged. 'You know I don't like standing still. I'd rather be doing something.'

'I thought you'd gone home,' confessed Liv. 'I didn't think you'd hung around.'

Ryan shot her an odd look.'Why would I go home? What- just because you told me to go?' he laughed and shook his head. 'Have I ever listened to you before? You were getting narky. So I thought I'd leave you to it. I know how much you like these rotten old places.' Ryan shivered and looked around. 'I still don't like it that much. I didn't want to come back down, to be honest. Then you disappeared.' He sat down beside her. 'Truth be told, Liv. I was a bit worried about you.' He looked into her eyes, searching for something. 'You were getting really freaky. When I saw you over here, I could hear you shouting something about knives. I thought you were going to stab me.' He looked down. 'I was really worried, actually. You kind of went for me. But it was a pen you had in your hand. Look.' He showed her his forearm. The day's sun had tanned his skin to a pinky-brown and tiny hairs shone golden across it. It did something funny to Liv's stomach. Then he turned his arm over and showed her a long streak of black ink stretching from the inside of his wrist to his elbow. The nib of the pen had made a tiny puncture wound in his flesh and the edges of the scratch were red and sore-looking. It was raised up and still painful to the touch. Ryan was grateful that the gash hadn't gouged out a deep channel up his arm– the black mark was very near the pale blue veins.

Liv gasped and took hold of his arm, staring at it. 'I did that?' she asked, horrified. 'Just now?' She looked up at him, embarrassed and contrite. 'Oh, Ryan! I'm so, so sorry. God, I could have really hurt you.'

'Well it did sting a bit,' smiled Ryan. He was lying. It had hurt him really badly. It didn't feel like a pen. It had felt like a real blade, dragging through his skin. It had taken him a few moments to realise it wasn't a knife blade and there wasn't any blood gushing down his arm. Nevertheless, when it had happened, he had yelped and pushed Liv roughly away from him. That's how she had gotten tangled up in her shoelaces and fallen down. He was worried that she'd banged her head. It was instinct that made him douse her with water to try and wake her up properly. He had read somewhere that you shouldn't wake a sleepwalker. But what did you do when she was yelling stuff at you that didn't make sense and shouting something that sounded like, 'Hey! Hey! You can't stay here!' Liv didn't come with a manual. He didn't always know the right thing to do with her. But he thought that, in general, he was pretty clued up on what made her tick and what chived her off. Chocolate. Chocolate was usually pretty good. That was why he'd decided to visit the man with the coffee cart in the car park, before he went back down to the temple. If he came to her bearing chocolate, it usually put her in a better mood. He'd been out of luck; the man didn't have any chocolate. But he'd got a packet of biscuits for her instead and hoped they would do the trick. That's when he saw her acting like a loon and decided to go and stop it. And then she attacked him. She'd been totally out of it though. Perhaps she had desperately needed a sugar fix after all.

'Um, I got you some biscuits?' he tried, rustling around in his back pocket. He shifted position slightly and brought them out. He handed them to her, flushing as he saw the state of the packet and hoping she wouldn't notice.

'You've sat on them,' said Liv, taking them from him. 'They're all crumbly.'

'Sorry,' he muttered.

''S OK,' Liv muttered back. She made a pretence of studying the biscuits just so he couldn't see her face properly. This day was too weird. Had she dreamt it all then? Fallen asleep while she was writing her notes about the temple and wandered in a daze over to the Well? And here was Ryan being as sweet and as stupid and as thoughtful as ever; and she'd physically attacked him. The guilt made her feel terrible. Her heart twisted as she thought of Marcus and remembered feeling his guilt at harming Aemelia. Worse than that. Marcus had killed Aemelia, hadn't he? That's the impression she got anyway. Was that what had kept him here? The guilt?

'I didn't mean to hurt you,' Liv said, finding it difficult to say the words. 'It was a mistake. You know that, don't you? I wouldn't have done it intentionally...' She clamped her lips together. There were those words again – it was a mistake.

Would people always be paying for their mistakes? And why did they hurt people they cared about?

'I know,' said Ryan. He sounded surprised. 'No need to apologise, Liv. You've done worse than draw on me with a pen before: joke!' he said, holding his hands up as Liv snapped her head up to face him, her eyes flashing. Then just as quickly, her anger died down and she gave a small sigh.

'It's OK. I probably have,' she said. 'And you're sure it wasn't snowing?' Her eyes searched his and he could tell she wanted him to confirm it for some reason.

'I'm pretty sure,' he said carefully. 'It wasn't snowing when I was at the coffee van. And it wasn't snowing when I went for a wander. But then, it might be a kind of sub-climate down here. You know, like how the Gulf Stream makes bits of Northern Scotland really warm. Maybe we've got a sub-Gulf Stream. A Roman Gulf Stream; that makes it snow in the valley down here.' He looked around him at the still, warm afternoon. 'It's a definite possibility.'

'Shut up,' Liv said, unwrapping the biscuits. 'You're trying to make me feel better.' She offered him the pack and he took a collection of broken pieces of biscuit out of it, laying them together like a jigsaw puzzle on his knee, making sure he hadn't been short-changed. When he was satisfied he had a whole biscuit, he began to eat it a piece at a time.

'You saw that man in the temple, didn't you?' asked Liv after a few moments. 'You said he'd been standing next to me.'

Ryan faltered in his munching. 'Yes. I thought I saw someone next to you,' he said carefully.

Liv nodded. 'I think I know who he is. Or was,' she said.

'What are you trying to say?' asked Ryan. The biscuit was suddenly tasteless and he laid it down.

'Don't laugh at me,' started Liv, 'but I think it was Marcus. You know. The guy who had the altar made?'

'What makes you say that?' asked Ryan. He laughed weakly and a pathetic attempt at humour escaped him. 'Did he tell you?' It was an even more pathetic attempt to cover up his nervousness; part of him didn't even want to hear Liv's answer.

'No,' said Liv slowly. Ryan relaxed. Then Liv spoke again. 'Meggie told me.'

'Liv! You are. You're mad as a box of frogs!' cried Ryan. 'That's just a legend. Meggie never existed. She's someone they made up, some old hag they thought was a witch...'

'Don't call her a hag!' cried Liv. To Ryan's horror, Liv burst into tears. 'She's not a hag. She's just a girl. Just a teenage girl, like me. Like Alice. And like Aemelia...' Then she began to shake uncontrollably. 'She wasn't a witch. And I couldn't save her and I couldn't help her and they would have taken me as well...And I saw her. I saw it happen in the temple. And it was horrible and nobody remembers her anymore. And nobody cared for her. And nobody believed her. And that man did all sorts of horrible things to her.'

Ryan stared at Liv, not knowing what to do. He'd never seen her dissolve like this before. She'd had tantrums and strops; but never proper crying. Never proper tears and stuff. He didn't like it. He stroked her shoulder awkwardly and this brought on a fresh onslaught of tears. Liv turned her body towards his and buried her head in his chest, grateful for the hard warmth of it, the living, beating heart that was buried beneath it.

'Oh Ryan. It's horrible. And I've been so horrible to you. I tried to stab you and it wasn't you, it was Charles Hay. And Marcus and Aemelia. They've got so much to sort out. She wouldn't listen to him, and it was all a mistake. And it was snowing at the Well and I saw them all. And I'm part of it, Ryan. I made it happen today. Meggie said so. And I want to come back to my life and to have you and everyone, but I don't want to leave her here on her own...' She gulped, choking back sobs, rubbing her wet face against his t-shirt. Ryan raised his arm and it hovered over her back for a moment. Then he lowered it and curled it around her shoulders, pulling her close to him, closing his eyes and smelling her hair and wondering if this was what it would be like for them, if they ever managed to get it together properly.

'Um. I think maybe you were dreaming?' said Ryan, patting her ineffectually. 'Why don't you have your biscuit?' He cursed himself as soon as he said it. That wasn't the time to be encouraging her to eat biscuits. It was the time to pull her in a little closer and try to find her mouth with his and kiss her until she felt better.

Ryan had nothing to lose. He decided to do just that. He eased away from Liv a little and took her face in his hands.

'But you know, you don't have to have your biscuit,' he said quietly. 'I can think of something else that might help.' He searched her face with his eyes, hoping to see some sort of assent in her gaze. She held his eyes for a moment, not quite understanding. Then she realised. She smiled at him and raised her own hands to her face, covering his. She slid her hands down his arms, gently pulling him towards her. She could feel the tiny, prickly hairs now, the hard biceps under his tee-shirt; the rough edges of the scratch on his forearm.

'I'm sorry about your arm,' she said. 'Really.'

'Sssh,' whispered Ryan. 'It's OK. It didn't hurt. Much.' Despite herself, Liv giggled and slid her arms up to his shoulders. Their faces were practically touching and Liv closed her eyes. There was no thought that this was 'only Ryan', like she had felt in the past. It felt right; right that they should be together now at this sacred place, right that she should be so close to touching his lips.

*She is an Enchantrix! She is a charmer!*

The words rose up out of the earth around them and echoed around the valley. They sprang apart as if a gun had fired.

'Liv!' cried Ryan. 'Did you hear that? What's happening?' They scrambled to their feet, some sixth sense warning them to run. Ryan reached out to grab Liv's hand and then he let out a scream of such agony and shock, that Liv began to scream as well. Something tore out of the remains of Coventina's Well, encircling the boy and lifting him off his feet. A black cloud surrounded him and Liv could see him through the mist, thrashing about, trying to right himself.

'Ryan!' Liv yelled. The black mist thickened and swirled, wrapping Ryan up in its grasp. 'Put him down! Stop it!' The black mist hung for a second as if it was mocking her, then it became thicker, squeezing itself around Ryan like a boa constrictor. Liv could hear Ryan coughing and choking, she saw his eyes wide and terrified. Then the mist pulled away from him, and spat him out onto the ground. He lay in a crumpled heap and Liv ran towards him. The black fog whooshed away from him and gusted past her, knocking her on to the ground.

'Ryan!' she gasped, dragging herself to her feet. She ran over to him, and threw herself down beside him. 'Ryan – can you hear me?' she cried, touching his face and stroking his hair. There was no response. 'Ryan!' She grabbed his shoulders and shook him. Ryan's eyes rolled back in his head and Liv screamed and another sound joined it; a horrible laughter which faded into the distance. Liv spun around, trying to catch a glimpse of whatever was with them in the valley.

'Stay away from me, Witch,' growled a voice.

Liv jumped to her feet.'Who is this?' she sobbed, looking around her wildly. More laughter. Then she heard Ryan groan and roll over onto his side. 'Ryan! Are you all right?'

Ryan curled his body into the foetal position and began murmuring something incomprehensible. Liv dropped down to the ground and bent over him, straining to hear what he was saying.

'Stay away from me,' he mumbled. 'Stay away from me. Witch. Enchantrix. Charmer.'

'Ryan! No! What are you saying...?' began Liv. Then Ryan uncoiled like a spring. He thrust his hand out and grabbed Liv, winding his fingers through the dark hair and pulling her roughly down towards him. She screamed and tried to yank herself free, but he had her trapped. His fingers brushed her cheek and she shuddered; they felt clammy and damp against her skin, her hair felt as if it was being torn out at the roots.

The awful laughter bubbled up again around her, and she realised it was coming from Ryan. He was strong. He held her fast so she was trapped there on her knees. His breath rasped against her neck and she began to panic. This wasn't Ryan. He would never do anything like this to her. The answer came to her in a flash, just like the images Meggie had shown her.

'Hay!' she choked out. 'Leave me alone!' She twisted her head around painfully, and she caught sight of Ryan through the tangle of her hair. His eyes were pure black; there was no definition between the pupil and the iris and Liv knew that it wasn't Ryan who was staring back at her.

Ryan laughed again, shaking his head. 'Why would I leave you alone?' he hissed. 'I never left any of them, even when they begged me to stop. You're mine now.'

'Ryan! No! You don't know what you're doing...' Liv felt her hair pull as Ryan balled his hand, grasping it into a fist. Then he shoved her over onto the grass. Liv fell awkwardly and cried out in pain. 'Please, no!' She sobbed. I'm not who you think I am,' she tried desperately.

Ryan laughed again, a harsh, grating sound.'I know exactly who you are,' he sneered. 'You're one of them.'

Liv felt a cold, sharp point at her throat and gasped. She didn't need to see it, to know it was the bone-handled knife.

'Ryan – no!' she cried.

# 2010

Liv felt the sharp point of the knife press into her throat. It wasn't a big knife, but it could easily puncture an artery. She was lying on her back and Ryan had his knee across her chest. He pressed down on her arm with his other hand, holding her with inhuman strength. Ryan raised the knife in the air, and Liv knew he was going to bring it down and pierce her skin.

It never ends, she thought, the evil never ends…

Ryan roared and Liv cried out, squeezing her eyes shut and waiting for the inevitable. Then suddenly she felt the pressure lift off her chest and Ryan was flung off her, rolling into a heap on the side of the boggy ground by the Well. There was a tiny clatter as the knife rolled out of his hand and bounced off a rock.

Through her closed eyelids, Liv saw a shimmering rainbow of light and felt cool hands touching her hair.

'She's all right,' said a voice. 'He hasn't harmed her.' The soft Northumbrian burr was unmistakeable.

'Meggie..' whispered Liv. 'Meggie?'

'Sssh, yes, Olivia. It's me,' replied Meggie. 'We have to be quick – he's going to get up in a minute. Aemelia can't hold him back for long.'

Liv scrambled to her feet and found she was looking into Meggie's clear grey eyes again.

'He's getting stronger,' said Meggie. 'He's using the boy's body and mind. It's not your friend who is lying there.'

'But if that's Hay, where's Ryan?' cried Liv. She saw the boy rolling on the ground in agony and shouting out. He looked as if he was trying to fight whatever was in him. Aemelia was standing over him, an invisible shield holding him in place by the Well. 'Why did Hay come back?' asked Liv. She ran forward towards Ryan and Aemelia.

'Stay away, Olivia!' commanded Aemelia. She turned her face to Liv, her dark eyes frightened. 'He is getting stronger.' Ryan rolled onto his front and arched his back. He glared up at Liv. She could see his face changing and distorting, as if Ryan was trying to come back and batter Hay into the boggy ground. Ryan - or Hay - shouted out a stream of obscenities and began to crawl across the grass towards Liv. Liv backed away, and Meggie slipped herself in between the two teenagers. She watched Ryan like a lioness ready to pounce. He bounced off the invisible shield and tumbled over onto his side again. He raked around on the ground, looking for the knife. Unable to find it, he was up on his feet, punching at the shield, trying to break out of it. Ripples of light rolled out, away from his fist as he pounded against the energy.

'We didn't make the circle properly,' Meggie said. 'Hay broke it before it had a chance to connect our energies. We have to try again. It's the only way we can stop his evil from infecting this place.'

'But I cannot leave Hay to join you!' cried Aemelia. 'If I move from here, he will attack Olivia.' Liv could see the energy around Aemelia breaking up; splinters of light like shooting stars were falling to the ground and sputtering on the grass.

'We have to do it,' said Liv, staring at Ryan. 'We have to take the chance. If we move quickly…'

'Hay can move more quickly,' countered Aemelia. 'Trust me. Meggie...?' Her voice tailed off.

'Olivia is right. We have to try,' said Meggie. Her voice was tight. She moved silently to Aemelia and took her hand. Meggie glanced around them. Her eyes fixed on a group of tall, green plants. Tiny, white, fluffy flowers like daisies burst out from the top of each stem. 'Yarrow,' she murmured. 'The devil's nettle – bloodwort. It will give us courage and boost our powers. It will help drive Hay's spirit out of the boy. The soldiers of Carrawburgh would have used it to staunch the bleeding. And Solomon's Seal.' She spotted a plant with arching stems and white, bell-like flowers drooping from it. Meggie smiled. 'That will also help the rid the boy of the spirit. It will bind our scared oath; the temple itself might have been consecrated with it. Yarrow and Solomon's Seal are all we have to help us. They will have to do. Sweet Olivia,' she said, turning to face Liv and holding her other hand out. 'You have to be brave. Can you do it?'

Liv nodded, and moved towards the Guardians of the Well. She was scared; so scared. A sob caught in her throat. Ryan snarled at her from his invisible prison and threw himself against it again.

'Oh Ryan,' Liv whispered. 'I'm sorry. I'm so sorry I made you come here.'

'We have to join hands,' said Meggie. 'Are you ready, my angels? We must do it…now!'

Aemelia took a last, frantic look at Ryan and turned her back on him, quickly grabbing Liv's hand. There was a whooshing sound and Ryan burst out of his makeshift gaol. He hurled himself towards the girls shouting and Liv began to scream.

# 2010

Liv saw Ryan hurtling towards her and tried to pull away from the group of three.

'Quickly!' shouted Meggie. 'We can do it…'

'Hold our hands, Olivia!' called Aemelia. 'Concentrate.'

Liv instinctively ducked as Ryan came flying at her and her hand slipped away from Meggie's. Aemelia and Meggie began shouting instructions at her, but their words were lost as a wild wind gusted up around them.

Then down from the fort, a rolling ball of light plunged towards them. It moved fast – faster even than the black ball of fury that was Hay masquerading as Ryan. It smashed into Ryan and enveloped him in a golden light. Liv saw Ryan's eyes open wide then he slumped inside the ball, which carried him back to the Well and hovered a few centimetres above the ground. The black and gold colours swirled around each other, sometimes the gold enveloping the black; sometimes the black seeping into the gold.

'He has come to help us,' whispered Aemelia. She sounded surprised. Then she turned to Meggie and Liv and raised her hands. Her voice powerful and strong again. 'Come. Olivia, take my hand. Let us complete the circle. He will hold him back. He is better than Hay.' There was a note of pride in her words as she looked fleetingly at the ball of black and gold light.

Liv wanted to ask who exactly was there, but instead she nodded and grabbed hold of Aemelia's hand. She clutched at Meggie's, interlocking her fingers tightly. Liv closed her eyes and took a deep breath. Aemelia began to speak.

'To the spirits and deities of this sacred place, I offer the water of protection from the blessed Well of Coventina and its Guardians. Stop the flow of negative energy from the ground below us, the air above us and the flames deep inside the earth. Send the negativity back to its source. Let it harm nothing and nobody on its course, and bind it within your power for all eternity. Let it never cause pain again.'

Liv felt the fizzing begin in her fingertips. The energy began slowly, encircling the group with streaks of silver. There was that humming in Liv's ears and a sound like men chanting. Then there were screams and images flashing into her mind again, whizzing back through the centuries like someone had pressed the rewind button. Liv opened her eyes and stared around her, her heart beating quickly. She felt one of the spirits squeeze her hand gently.

'It will soon be over. We are here with you.'
The words filled her thoughts, damming the tide of
panic that was welling up inside her. The landscape
was changing and altering before her eyes, like a
speeded up film. The layers of time were peeling
back and she was a witness to everything that had
gone before her.

There were the modern day tourists, the
walkers and backpackers. There were the council
men, building the modern road on top of the ruins
of the wall. She saw the fields dry and yellow in a
blistering hot summer; the tops of the altars in the
temple poking out of the ground. Now, the
landscape was green; the temple disappearing
beneath the meadow flowers. Animals grazed
peacefully, unaware of the grass growing up over
the temple walls and burying it. Now groups of
people in Victorian dress crowded around the Well;
one policeman directing them away from the stone
walls which surrounded it; an elderly man held
court, passing trinkets around the spectators. The
temple was hidden now beneath the moorland;
nobody knew it was there any more. The scene
darkened; groups of lead miners swarmed over the
land, ransacking trays left behind overnight. Further
back again, and a young girl fell to her knees before
a Witchfinder; a hazy figure walked towards her
through the middle of the derelict temple. Liv
gasped, recognising it.

'It's all right, it's all right,' whispered a voice. 'We have to see this.'

'No! No, I don't want to see you get hurt!' cried Liv.

But then it was gone. Further back, and shadows of men played out the destruction of the temple and the Well. Then it was back to when the vicus was bustling with activity, with people milling around the market, throwing coins into the Well and laughing.

Liv saw men building the fort and the temple and the Well, working in all weathers to construct them. And then it was silent. The landscape was bleak and empty, but for a light snow fall which covered everything in white and a sky which glowed pink and orange.

The images faded and Liv wobbled. Her head was pounding and tears were pouring down her face.

'So much history,' she said, her voice catching. 'So much...'

'It's our history,' said Meggie. 'And we have been charged with protecting it.' She smiled at Liv and reached out to brush her fingers over the girl's wet cheeks. 'You're part of it, Olivia. You can feel that, can't you?'

Liv nodded.'I wish I could have changed things,' she said. 'For you.'

'These things have to happen. I see that now,' smiled Meggie. 'It's beyond our power to change any of it. And I'm at peace. Really I am. I have found my place and I embrace it.'

'But what about Aemelia? What was her story?' asked Liv.

'Aemelia was like me. She was a means to an end. She had no control over it, and neither did Marcus.' Meggie laid her hand on Liv's shoulder. 'I'm pleased you were spared that vision. She worked hard to keep it from you. Believe me; it was worse than mine.' Liv opened her mouth but shut it quickly. The questions were bubbling up inside her, but mad as it sounded, she trusted Meggie. She knew that whatever had happened to Aemelia, it was too painful for her to share. All she knew was that it had something to do with Marcus. And whatever it was, it had tormented him for centuries. She looked around to speak to the dark eyed girl to reassure her that her secret was safe.

Aemelia was walking slowly towards the Well. A column of light was hovering around the marshland. Aemelia stopped in front of the column and it wavered, then glowed brighter. Liv blinked as it sparkled like a string of diamonds.

'Corpse candles,' breathed Liv, remembering something Ryan had told her years ago, one Halloween. 'It's like a corpse candle. Ryan said it was marsh gases – but that's not marsh gas is it?' Meggie shook her head.

'No. It's not,' she said quietly.

'What is it? And where's Ryan? Where's he gone?'

'Ryan is safe. Look- can you see him behind the light?' Ryan was sitting down, his head on his knees, his arms wrapped around them. Liv could see he was trembling, even from this distance. She wanted to run over to him, but she hesitated. She didn't know what the light was. What if it was Hay again?

'Don't worry; it can't harm us,' smiled Meggie, reading her. 'You've seen what these will o' the wisps really are now, Olivia. Some people think they are an omen of death. This one,' she nodded at it, 'is a spirit that has found peace. Can you feel it?' Liv stood very still and concentrated. She felt a sort of solace washing over her, and opened her eyes wide as she made out a figure within the column. The column and the figure merged into one and the man who appeared walked over to Aemelia. Hesitantly, he offered her his hand. Aemelia paused for a second, then took it. They drew closer to one another, silhouetted against the landscape, as the man bent down and took her face in his hands.

'It's Marcus,' she whispered. 'That's him, isn't it? He's made peace with himself.'

'And he's made peace with Aemelia,' said Meggie, following Liv's gaze. 'He's proved himself to her at last. He's free to move on now.'

'But he's not going to, is he?' asked Liv. 'He's part of this as much as you are. If Aemelia has to stay here, he'll want to be with her. She's a Guardian.'

'Yes, but she can choose as well. She can move freely now. She's not trapped here either. It was her anger and disbelief that held her back. But I know Aemelia. She'll want to return. And she can. But she doesn't have to stay here. Not anymore.'

'But you will. You'll have to stay, won't you?' said Liv, wrapping her arms around herself. 'And you'll have nobody if Aemelia goes with Marcus...' she felt the tears well up again, imagining Meggie wandering around these wild lands all alone. Meggie turned to Liv, and again there was that cool, ethereal touch on her hair as Meggie comforted her.

'But I was always free to go, Olivia,' she said. 'I chose to stay here.'

'But..?' asked Liv, staring at her. 'I thought...'

Meggie smiled.'I made my peace long ago. I accepted what had happened. I knew it was my fault that Alice had died. I was always drawn to this place.' She looked around her, squinting slightly into the distance at something Liv couldn't see. 'I'm happy. My other life was lonely and harsh and I can't even begin to describe it. I had nobody. When Alice went...' Meggie shrugged. 'I didn't want to be there anymore. She was the only one who understood. I was too different from the rest of them. But they didn't care; it was only when they wanted me for something that they'd come and find me. And then, it was all so secretive. I only wanted to help people. You believe me, don't you?'

Liv nodded.'So all this time, you could have been somewhere else. Like...like Heaven or something?' she asked.

Meggie laughed. 'Yes. Like Heaven or something. I can still go there, don't worry. And I can be with Alice there. But this place. This place is my true Heaven. I'm part of it. And so are you now. Oh look,' she indicated Ryan. The two figures had faded away, leaving Ryan alone. 'I think you need to check your friend. He needs you. See him?'

'Ryan!' shouted Liv. She dashed off towards him, squelching her way through the boggy ground.

# 2010

Ryan was sitting hunched up on a dry part of the grass, staring all about him. His face was white and drawn and Liv could see that he was still trembling. She hunkered down next to him and touched his knee. Ryan flinched.

'It's OK, Ryan, it's OK. It's only me,' she said gently. 'You're safe now. He's gone.'

'What happened?' asked Ryan. His voice was shaky. 'It's all fuzzy in my head. One minute I'm sitting next to you and the next...' He looked at her and gave a humourless, lopsided smile. 'It must have been one hell of a kiss,' he said, his voice strange and flat. 'Probably serves me right. Probably shouldn't have tried. I...'

The rest of his sentence was smothered. Liv leaned over and kissed him hard on the lips. Ryan gave a little gurgle of shock, then found himself responding. He was hesitant at first; then as he found his confidence, he kissed her with a mixture of eagerness and desperation. He reached his arms up and locked them behind Liv's neck. She wrapped her arms around his waist and they stayed entwined, lost in each other, as the atmosphere around them became still again.

'Wow,' said Ryan, gazing at Liv. 'I'm sorry. I can't come up with anything clever to say. Just...wow.'

Liv laughed, a little self-consciously.'Yeah. I know what you mean,' she said. 'Wow. Who would have thought it?'

'But you haven't explained what happened,' said Ryan. 'Before. When all that fuzzy stuff was going on. I'm sorry, Liv. But I really can't remember any of it.'

'You really can't can you?' she said quietly, watching him. 'Nothing. There's nothing there.'

'Not a thing. Liv, this place is weird. I know I said that earlier, but I've decided I really don't like it. There's something here... I don't even know if it wants us to be here.' He looked around again, concerned that whatever 'it' was might still be lurking in the undergrowth. Liv sat back and picked idly at the plants around her. She snapped off a flower and turned it over in her hands, looking at the tiny, daisy-shaped flowers.

'Yarrow,' she said. 'The devil's nettle. Do you know something, Ryan? There's so much we don't understand in this life. I wonder if it all sorts itself out...afterwards. You know?'

'What? Like when we're dead?' said Ryan, looking askance at her. He shook his head. 'I don't know. You're starting to freak me out a bit, I have to say. Again. You're freaking me out: again.'

Liv looked at him and half-smiled. 'I'm not going into detail with you,' she said. 'But you do that to me as well, you know. You've freaked me out before now.' Ryan pulled his knees up to his chest and dropped his head onto them.

He closed his eyes.'Come on. Something weird happened, didn't it? I didn't just lose half an hour did I?' Liv could see his shoulders tensing up, waiting for her to confirm it. She stroked his back and felt a little shiver run down his spine through her fingers. She smiled to herself. Yes. Who would have thought it?

'Yes. Something weird did happen, Ryan,' she said. She thought for a moment. Maybe one day she would tell him. But would he really, truly appreciate being told he'd been possessed by a mad seventeenth century rapist, hell-bent on revenge? Or that she'd saved this sacred place and the spirits that lingered here, by joining hands with two ghosts - two Guardians of this wild, beautiful landscape? Or maybe there were three Guardians now? This time she shivered. She was inextricably linked to this place; that was for sure. 'And it's going to get even weirder,' she said, looking at him. The edge of his hair curled gently against his collar and she moved her fingers up to stroke it. It was smooth and springy beneath her touch.

'How? How can it get weirder?' asked Ryan, looking up at her. His eyebrows knitted together. 'Come on. I'm not stupid. This whole place has been weird. All day. You stabbed me with that pen. And you went crazy. And we both saw...weird things. And now I've got a fuzzy head and I can't remember anything since we sort of didn't kiss.'

'Can you not remember properly kissing just now?' teased Liv.

'You're not answering the question,' argued Ryan. 'Of course I can remember that one. It's just before that. It's fuzzy.'

Liv half smiled.'Yeah, well. It's got to stay fuzzy. I don't know what happened myself.'

'Liar,' said Ryan.

'Yup,' said Liv. 'But you wouldn't believe me anyway.'

'Try me.'

'No.'

Liv raised her eyes and scanned the area for Meggie. She half expected her to be standing on the edge of the field, or hovering by the temple. Or even watching them from Carrawburgh. But she wasn't there. She'd gone. And so had Aemelia: and Marcus. All gone.

Liv sighed. She couldn't even feel them around her anymore. They'd come back though. They were bound to the place. As she was. She sat up, stretching her arms out behind her to lean back on her hands. Under one of them, she felt a hard, sharp object. Her stomach flipped; she could tell by the shape of it that it was the knife. She cast a glance at Ryan. He had his head on his knees again. Carefully, she eased the knife into her hand and curled it inside her fist. They were quite near to Coventina's Well. Liv silently judged the distance to it from where she sat; not far. She flicked her wrist and let go of the knife, sending it somersaulting towards the Well. There was a tiny splash and the knife sank into the filthy water, to be swallowed up by the mud at the bottom of the spring. Liv let out her breath; she hadn't even realised she was holding it.

Ryan turned to her, the tiny splash startling him out of his reverie. 'You won't tell me, will you?' he said.

'Damn right,' she replied.

'Well. In that case, would you kiss me again?' Then there it was; that irresistible twinkle was back in his eye. 'Because I don't actually believe you did that either.'

Liv grinned at him, her heart suddenly lighter. 'Damn right I'll kiss you again,' she said. 'I'll let you believe that one.'

The End

THE MEMORY OF SNOW

**By the same author**

## REFUGE

A legendary dagger in the hands of a vampire
slayer...
A nineteenth century girl with nowhere left to turn...
A modern day field trip to Lindisfarne...

When worlds collide and the only way out is a
choice nobody should have to make, where do you
find your refuge?
Set within the sanctity of the Holy Island of
Lindisfarne, off the Northumbrian coast, Refuge is a
story interlinking modern day with a dark and
terrifying past – and the story of the immortals who
carry their hatred with them throughout the
centuries.

**www.rosethornpress.co.uk**

Printed in Great Britain
by Amazon